# Love Inspired
## SUSPENSE
### RIVETING INSPIRATIONAL ROMANCE

# MIA:
## MISSING
## IN ATLANTA

## DEBBY
## GIUSTI

POLICE

Steeple Hill®

Cindy Rosso

Steeple
Hill®

**Riveting Inspirational Suspense**

ISBN-13:978-0-373-44284-3
ISBN-10: 0-373-44284-X

⬦ EAN

**LOVE INSPIRED
SUSPENSE®
TITLES AVAILABLE
THIS MONTH:**

**WILDFIRE**
*Snow Canyon Ranch*
Roxanne Rustand

**DON'T LOOK BACK**
*Reunion Revelations*
Margaret Daley

**BROKEN LULLABY**
Pamela Tracy

**MIA: MISSING IN ATLANTA**
Debby Giusti

**The danger past, Sarah slumped
with relief. If Jude hadn't arrived
when he did—**

He was staring at her. She saw concern in his eyes, but
his voice was stern. "Did he hurt you?"

She shook her head. "I...I'm fine. Thanks to you."

The light from the porch caught the set of his jaw. "It
was foolish to come outside."

She bristled. She'd realized her mistake, but didn't
want to admit she'd been wrong. "I was worried about
the safety of the girls inside."

"Yeah, well, locking the door and staying inside would
have been smarter. You put yourself in danger. I was
worried, Sarah."

Jude's face softened. A strand of hair fell over her
cheek. He reached out and tucked it behind her ear.

His touch sent a chill down Sarah's spine that had
nothing to do with fear and had everything to do with
the man standing in front of her.

## Books by Debby Giusti

Love Inspired Suspense

*Nowhere To Hide* #49
*Scared To Death* #66
*MIA: Missing in Atlanta* #94

## *DEBBY GIUSTI,*

a born and raised army brat, is a medical technologist who loves working with test tubes and petri dishes almost as much as she loves to write. Debby met and married her husband— then a captain in the army—at Fort Knox, Kentucky. Together they traveled the world, raised three wonderful army brats of their own and have now settled in Atlanta, Georgia, where Debby spins tales of suspense that touch the heart and soul.

Contact Debby through her Web site, www.DebbyGiusti.com, by e-mail debby@debbygiusti.com or c/o Steeple Hill, 233 Broadway, Suite 1001, New York, NY 10279.

# MIA: MISSING IN ATLANTA

## DEBBY GIUSTI

Steeple Hill®

Published by Steeple Hill Books™

STEEPLE HILL BOOKS

Steeple
Hill®

ISBN-13: 978-0-373-44284-3
ISBN-10:    0-373-44284-X

MIA: MISSING IN ATLANTA

www.SteepleHill.com

**Printed in U.S.A.**

You are forgiving and good, O Lord,
abounding in love to all who call to you.
—*Psalms* 86:5

This book is dedicated to:

Captain Joseph Giusti
Colonel Anthony Giusti
Colonel Glen Willoughby
My son, my husband, my father—my heroes!

The soldiers of the 101st Airborne Division
(Air Assault)
And all the brave men and women
in uniform who defend our nation.
God bless you for your service to our country.

Liz, Mary Katie, Eric and Anna
For your love and support.

Darlene Buchholz, Annie Oortman,
Dianna Snell, Sharon Yanish and Connie Gillam
Thank you!

My editor Jessica Alvarez
And my agent Deidre Knight
For your guidance and wise counsel.

# ONE

Not what he expected.

Captain Jude Walker fingered the scrap of paper and, once again, glanced at the address Nicole had sent him—114 Rosemont Avenue.

It'd been seven days since the 101st Airborne had redeployed home from the Middle East, and this was his first opportunity to leave Fort Campbell. The last mandatory reintegration briefing had ended at noon. He'd signed out on two-weeks' leave, climbed into his pickup and headed to Atlanta. Four hours later here he sat on Rosemont.

Tension tightened his shoulders, and a wave of anxiety rolled through his gut. He felt as if he was in a combat zone instead of this residential city street. It was probably the worry that had eaten at him for a month or so.

Why had Nicole stopped answering his e-mails? A glitch with her Internet provider, or so she'd claimed over the phone. The last time they'd talked, she assured him her system would be back online within a day or two.

He would have believed her except for the apprehension he'd heard in her voice.

"What's wrong, Nicole?"

"Nothing, baby. Everything's gonna be fine."

Three days later, a lone message appeared in his inbox, compounding his unease. "Don't try to find me."

Then her phone had been disconnected….

Almost five weeks and nary a word.

His military training had taught him to plan for the worst-case scenario. He'd called every hospital in the Atlanta area, just in case. The long-distance charge had been worth his peace of mind. No one named Nicole Valentine had been admitted to a medical facility in the metro area.

The police had been less than forthcoming, except to assure Jude a missing persons report had not been submitted in her name.

Foolish as it seemed, Jude had talked himself into believing she'd be waiting for him when his plane touched down at Fort Campbell. A crowd of exuberant well-wishers swarmed the tarmac, waving American flags and screaming with joy as he and his men deplaned. He searched the crowd but never found Nicole.

Standing alone when every other man had someone to wrap his arms around had been worse than marching into battle. The sense of emptiness haunted him still.

Jude let out a breath of frustration. Had he read too much into their chance meeting in Atlanta? Without a family to go home to and knowing he'd be assigned to Atlanta's Fort McPherson shortly after his thirteen-months' deployment was over, Jude had chosen the city as a good spot to visit over R&R in the middle of his stint. Meeting Nicole had been a plus he'd never expected.

The two weeks passed quickly as they got to know each other. Nicole seemed enthusiastic about their relationship until he happened to mention the possibility of a future together.

"Gotta live in the moment," she quipped when the subject came up. "Besides, you don't know me. You don't know who I really am."

"I know enough," he assured her. But the truth was, he didn't know anything about Nicole except she'd been staying at the same hotel. Unusual, yes, since she lived in Atlanta. A minivacation without leaving town, she claimed.

At that point he'd been too taken in by her warm smile and twinkling eyes to question anything.

But now, after being deployed for thirteen months, the last thing he needed was rejection.

Surely everything would work out once they were together again.

And what about her e-mail that warned him not to try to find her? Merely anxiety on her part about reconnecting after six months? At least that's what he kept telling himself.

Bracing for whatever would unfold, Jude grabbed his beret and stepped onto the pavement, wishing he'd taken time to change into civilian clothes. Hopefully, she'd be glad to see him, no matter what he was wearing.

Slamming the truck door, he glanced down Rosemont. An older neighborhood. At one time, probably prime real estate, now slightly in need of repair.

One-fourteen sat back from the road. A three-story rambling brick complete with a sprawling porch, two white wicker rockers and a pot of yellow pansies that waved a greeting as he neared. He imagined Nicole sitting in the rocker, awaiting his return.

Jude had faced combat, had known the caustic taste of bile that churned in his gut when danger needed to be faced. Not that he gave the fear control, but it was a presence, a shadow that hovered over any battlefield. Today he felt that same shadow float over him as the late-February sun slipped momentarily behind a dark and angry cloud.

An omen? Something Jude didn't believe in. A man controlled his destiny by the way he lived his life.

Still, he wasn't sure what he'd find on the other side of the door. The Nicole he'd met on R&R? Or a woman who had turned her back on the memory of their two weeks together?

Pulling in a calming breath, Jude walked toward the house. It'd been six months since they'd been together. Seemed like an eternity.

Sarah Montgomery cradled the phone on her shoulder, trying to keep the frustration from her voice. No reason for the head of the Caring Heart Foundation to know she was angry.

"Sir, I wasn't meddling. As acting director of Hope House, I was merely reviewing the records. When the figures didn't add up, I decided to dig a little deeper."

"You should have alerted me immediately, Sarah." Winton Cunningham's voice was stern.

"That's exactly what I am doing. Cynthia is due back at the end of the month. I wanted to ensure there were no problems before she returns."

Winton sighed. "Look, Sarah, the board appreciates the job you've done filling in as temporary director these past six months, but there's no reason to delve into money issues. We have credible people at the foundation who handle the finances. They do an outstanding job, and I trust their integrity."

"I wasn't implying—"

"Of course you weren't. But you must realize the stress everyone is under. Contributions are down, and the foundation's trying to hold Hope House together."

"Aren't you overexaggerating the situation?"

"Unfortunately, no. If a couple of our major contributors get wind of mismanaged funds, even if the story is unfounded—" Winton sniffed "—the consequences would be devastating. I'd hate to see Hope House close its doors because of a simple accounting error. So, you tend to the kids and let the foundation handle the money. Understand?"

Sarah's cheeks burned from the chastisement. "Of course."

"No need to mention this to the other board members tomorrow night at the Charity Ball. I don't want to spoil their evening. Plus, the last thing we need is bad PR. You know how the press loves to stick its nose where it doesn't belong."

"I hadn't planned to talk to anyone else about the situation, sir."

"Excellent. After dinner I'll invite you to the stage for the presentation. Accept the donation, then say a few words to the contributors."

"I understand."

"What about the application for the orphanage referral position? Have you submitted your paperwork?"

"It's in the mail." Sarah hesitated. "If the donations are down, won't that affect the project in South America?"

"Not at all. My wife, Elena, still has family in Colombia where she was raised. They're funding the project and insist their contributions remain separate from Hope House's resources. No matter what happens in Atlanta, they want the orphanage referral agency established so more South American children can be adopted by American families. Bottom line, the program will remain on schedule."

The stability of the Colombian project didn't make Sarah feel any better. As acting director of Hope House, her first priority was the kids in Atlanta.

She hung up the phone and sighed. If she hadn't noticed the discrepancy—

Well, she had noticed and look where it had gotten her. On the losing end of a verbal squabble with Mr. Cunningham.

The sound of a car door slamming pulled her from her thoughts. Shoving the curtain aside, she peered through her office window at the man in uniform walking purposefully toward the house.

Not the usual visitor by a long shot, with his black army beret angled over his forehead, squared shoulders and a determined look plastered on his chiseled face.

She tucked the curtain back in place as three knocks resounded though the house.

"Patience is a virtue," she muttered as a second repetition echoed like machine-gun fire. Obviously, the man didn't like to be kept waiting.

Stepping into the foyer, Sarah opened the front door to the extent of the chain lock and regarded the visitor.

Crystal-blue eyes, straw-blond hair cut in a military buzz.

When he turned those blue eyes toward her, a feeling stirred deep within her. She swallowed, having difficulty finding her voice.

Not what she needed at this point in her life. *Get a grip, Sarah.*

"May I help you?"

"Yes, ma'am."

Polite. She'd give him that much. Probably six-two, he had a thick neck, broad shoulders and biceps that bulged beneath the digital pattern of his uniform.

He glanced down at a photograph he clutched in his hand and held it up to where she could see the woman's image. Expressive round eyes, slender nose, shoulder-length black hair framing an oval face.

"Ma'am, I'm looking for Nicole Valentine."

No doubt the person in the photo. Sarah raised a questioning brow. "And you came here because…?"

He let out a quick breath. "One-fourteen Rosemont. That is your address, isn't it?"

"That's right, but—"

"Nicole Valentine lives here," he stated before Sarah could continue. Then he paused, probably noticing the perplexed expression on her face. "I just returned from the Middle East. Nicole and I…" He glanced again at the photo. "You see, ma'am, she sent me this address."

Sarah could read people, and everything about the man standing on her front porch said he was legit. Maybe a little mixed up as to where his girlfriend lived, but the guy didn't seem to pose a threat to either Sarah or the kids at the shelter.

"Just a minute." She slipped off the chain lock, opened the door wide and walked onto the porch.

He took a step back. Had she crowded him?

"Look, Major—"

His gaze warmed momentarily. "Hate to turn down a promotion, but it's captain, ma'am. Captain Jude Walker."

She nodded and tried to offer him what she realized must have seemed a halfhearted smile. But she did have work to do and kids to take care of, so…

"Captain Walker."

"Call me Jude, ma'am."

"And I'm Sarah Montgomery." The guy seemed sweet in a rugged sort of way, like a cocker spaniel in a rottweiler body.

"I'm afraid you have the wrong address, Jude. This is a shelter for teens. Your girlfriend doesn't live here."

"But—"

He hadn't corrected her when she called the beautiful woman his girlfriend. For half a heart-beat, Sarah envied the woman in the photo.

"A teen shelter? Are you sure?"

His question sounded like one the kids would ask. "Yes, I *am* sure, Captain. I'm well aware of who finds lodging within this house."

He tilted his head, a flash of irritation evident in his eyes.

She'd been too abrupt. Sarah sighed. Despite the phone call with Winton Cunningham and the financial reports that didn't add up, this man—this Jude Walker—deserved a few minutes of her time.

"Look, I'm sorry. That was harsh. It's been a rough day and…"

She stopped her explanation. No reason to tell the captain about the problem she'd uncovered.

Reaching for the picture, she gave it a long look. "What'd you say her name was?"

"Nicole Valentine."

A memory niggled at the back of Sarah's mind.

She glanced into his blue eyes, now hooded, as if her hasty comment had lowered a shield over the open heart he'd exposed earlier.

"Why don't you sit down for a minute?" She pointed to the wicker rocker. "I'll check the roster. I've worked here for about six months. Seems to me when I first arrived there was a girl named Valentine."

A flicker of hope flashed over his face. "Thank you, ma'am."

His sincerity touched her.

She started to step inside and then hesitated, noting the way he sighed with relief as he settled his body into the rocker.

"How long have you been back in the States?"

The sun played over his haunting eyes, and for the first time she saw the fatigue that lined his face.

"Seven days." He stretched his legs out in front of him.

How had all that length of man managed to stay contained in the crowded seat of an airliner for the long trip back from overseas?

"I don't know if anyone's told you yet, but a lot

of people in the United States appreciate what the military's doing."

"Just doing my job, ma'am."

Sure. The world could use more Jude Walkers.

"Give me a minute to look up those records."

She stepped into the house's warm interior and pulled the door shut behind her. For a moment she leaned against the hardwood frame. Something about the man tugged at her heart.

The accounting problems could wait. She'd give the captain a few minutes of her time before she sent him on his way. That was the least he deserved.

Jude tapped his foot and let out a frustrated breath. He appreciated the shelter worker's help, but he had expected Nicole to be the woman answering the door.

Not Sarah Montgomery.

Tall and fair-skinned with golden-brown hair. Around thirty. His age or a year or two younger. For all her attempts to be authoritative, she missed the mark. Compassion was what he saw staring back at him from her green eyes.

He scanned the sleepy neighborhood of older homes. Seemed like a safe environment. Not a bombed-out hovel in the lot of them. No bullet-scarred walls, no worry of land mines or IEDs or rocket launchers in enemy hands.

Hardly seemed to warrant a shelter.

Yet every city had areas where bad things happened. Inner-city crime. Street drugs. He may have been deployed for thirteen months but the facts of life remained. Every country had its problems.

Why had Nicole given him *this* address? Nothing made sense.

Jude glanced at his watch.

What was keeping Ms. Montgomery? Maybe she was calling the police and telling them about the weird guy in a rumpled uniform who had taken up residence on her front step.

A dull thud pounded in the deep recesses of his brain. Chalk it up to the worry that continued to eat at his gut.

Jude closed his eyes and thought of the way the dimples in the corners of Nicole's cheeks appeared when she laughed.

They had laughed so much. Deep, turn-your-world-topsy-turvy laughter that wiped away the past and gave him hope for the days ahead. Days he wanted to spend with Nicole.

The door creaked. He rose as Sarah stepped onto the porch.

"I checked the overnight log. A young woman named Viki Valentine stayed here for a couple weeks, six months ago. She left just a few days after I arrived."

"But what about Nicole? Perhaps she was a volunteer?"

"Not in the last six months."

Jude sighed. Nicole had mentioned a younger sister, although he couldn't remember her name. As much as he hated to think of someone in Nicole's family ending up in a shelter for wayward teens, even good kids made bad decisions that got them in trouble. "Do you know where I can find Viki?"

Sarah shook her head. "I'm afraid she left without telling anyone."

"You must keep records," Jude pushed.

"Of course, but only if the kids give us information."

The breeze blew a strand of hair across Sarah's cheek. She tugged it back into place and tilted her head as she stared back at him. "You've got to understand, Jude. Usually the kids who stay here have no place else to go. They run away from a bad life at home and run into a worse situation on the street."

"You're saying this Viki Valentine came from a troubled home?"

"More than likely. And for whatever reason, she didn't want to accept the help we offered."

"Any idea where I should *start* looking for her?"

Sarah hesitated, her face clouding for an instant. "Viki may have gone back to where we find a lot of the girls," she finally said. "The area's about six blocks from here. Head to Moreland Avenue and go south. At the fourth light make a right. You'll see a series of run-down motels. Some of the girls work the streets in that area."

"Work the streets?"

"That's right. Like so many of the girls we rescue, Viki Valentine is a prostitute."

# TWO

A streetlight glowed in the cold night air, throwing shadows across the faces of the people Jude passed. An empty cigarette pack littered the sidewalk along with fast-food wrappers and the want-ad section of the newspaper, all strewn like rubble across the cracked cement.

Rap music blasted a message of violence and despair from the stream of motorists who cruised the streets, looking for...?

Jude could only imagine.

A plastic bag of powder? Enough crank or ice or speed to drown out the reality of life on the street.

And what was Jude looking for? He'd pounded the pavement for hours, lost in his own world of unanswered questions. Did he really think he could find Nicole?

She was probably far from this area of unfulfilled dreams, living the good life that didn't include an army guy she'd met by chance at a coffee shop six months ago.

He let out an aggravated breath. Had he deluded himself, thinking fate had brought them together?

Nicole's take had been less romantic and more realistic.

"Baby, it's just that our paths crossed for a moment in time."

And then she'd moved on?

Is that why she'd given him the wrong address?

And what about her e-mail and disconnected phone service? Surely that was overkill.

Unless she was running away. From what?

A two-week relationship filled with the promise of developing into something more?

Jude tugged at his Windbreaker. The temperature had dropped significantly with the setting sun.

At least he'd changed into civilian clothes. No reason to advertise he was military. Plus he doubted people would be forthcoming talking to a man in uniform.

Up ahead two women leaned against a brick storefront, the display window covered in a protective web of wrought iron.

The taller of the two tapped her boots to ward off the cold, the tasseled suede covering more leg than the miniskirt that stopped midthigh. The other stood on red stiletto heels, legs wrapped in fishnet stockings. A thin slip of a dress hung on her bony body. She clutched a denim jacket around her shoulders and shivered in the night air.

Couldn't be more than fifteen. Pretty mocha face. Shoulder-length hair. Big eyes that turned as Jude approached.

Someone Sarah needed to take home to her shelter.

A late-model sedan pulled to the curb. Two guys, wearing sport coats and ties. The front-passenger window lowered.

Jude fisted his hands and hustled forward, realizing what the men were hoping to buy.

*Not the young one.*

The older woman climbed into the rear seat, and the car sped away into the night.

The girl left behind stared at Jude.

He dug in his back pocket and fished out his wallet. The least he could do was help. Palming three twenties, he cautiously approached the teen.

Doubtful she'd take the money without encouragement. Maybe he could trade for information.

"Miss?" Jude pulled Nicole's picture from his pocket. "I'm looking for someone." The girl glanced nonchalantly at the photo he held up to her.

Jude fingered the bills. "Have you ever seen this woman? Or someone named Viki Valentine?"

A flicker of recognition swept over her face.

"Do you know Viki?"

The girl grabbed the twenties. "Why you want Viki when you can have me? I be nice to you." She pushed off the brick wall and wiggled toward him. "First time you pick up a girl?"

Jude took a step back. "Look, miss, I'm not interested in buying anything from you except some information. Do you know where I can find Viki Valentine?"

The girl's eyes swept past Jude, her face caught in a pulse of light. A car door slammed. Jude glanced over his shoulder and squinted into the bright glare.

With a flash of motion, the young woman raced around the corner.

A police officer stepped onto the sidewalk. "Hold it right there, sir."

The officer mumbled something into the radio on his shoulder. The dispatcher squawked a reply.

Jude raised his right hand, palm out. "I was just talking to the girl."

"You gave her money."

"So she could get off the street and find a motel room." Bad choice of words. "You've got it all wrong, Officer. I wasn't making a buy or trying to pick up the girl. Besides, she couldn't be more than fifteen."

"Since when's that stopped anyone?" Sarcasm

was evident in the cop's voice. "Step to the car, sir. Put your hands on the hood."

"What?" The cop wasn't interested in Jude's side of the story. "I'm a captain in the army. I've been overseas for the last—"

"Lonely and lookin' for a woman, eh?"

"Actually, I am looking for a friend of mine."

"Friend or not, solicitation's against the law. Now, spread your legs, hands on the hood."

"Solicitation?" Jude let out an exasperated breath. "You don't understand."

"I understand you'll be cited with resisting arrest if you don't move. Now, buddy."

How had he gotten into this mess?

Jude clamped down on his jaw and held his anger in check as the cop patted him down. Arms, torso, both legs.

"Put your hands behind your back."

"Officer, this is entirely unnecessary," Jude said.

Cold steel cuffs snapped around his wrists. The night had gone from bad to worse.

On the opposite side of the street, a utility van pulled to the curb. The driver's door opened and a black man—probably six-four, three hundred pounds, gold ring hanging from his left earlobe— dodged the traffic and hustled toward them.

"Yo, Brian, my man. What's up?" The big guy high-fived the cop.

"Another john. Claims he was merely talking."

The newcomer eyed Jude. "What are you doing, boy? I told you we work outta the van. Last thing you want is to scare off the ladies."

Jude gave the guy a long, hard look. Who was he?

The officer cocked his brow. "This dude one of yours?"

"A little too zealous, but his heart's in the right place."

"He gave money to a young girl," the cop explained. "She ran off before I could talk to her."

The black man chuckled. "Now, Jude, how many times I tell you get 'em off the street before you go giving them handouts."

Okay. Jude shrugged. He'd play along. The last thing he needed was a solicitation charge on his military record. "I was trying to help."

"I hear ya. But right now, we need you back at the house." The newcomer looked at the cop. "You mind undoing the cuffs?"

He hesitated.

"Come on, Brian," said the big man. "My brother always said you were a good man."

"Not as good as he was." The officer sighed, then slapped Jude's shoulder. "Sorry, buddy. Guess I jumped to the wrong conclusion."

"No harm done." Jude rubbed his wrists, at last

free of the metal restraints. Close call, to say the least.

"Let's go." The big guy motioned him toward the van.

On the opposite side of the street, Jude stopped short. "Look, I appreciate your help, but—"

His rescuer eyed the cop, who had paused before getting into his squad car.

"Best get in the van or Brian'll think I'm a lying skunk. I can drop you at the next corner, if you like."

Jude glanced across the street. The police officer stared back at him.

Didn't take long to weigh his options. Jude stepped toward the van. Sliding open the side-panel door, he stared into the same green eyes he'd met earlier today.

"Sarah?"

"Get in," she said between clenched teeth.

Jude hoisted himself onto the rear bench, surprise written on his face.

She scooted over, giving him more room. "Don't hand money to *anyone* on the street."

His eyes narrowed. "Thanks for the advice. Like I told the cop, I was just trying to help."

"Which you weren't. That isn't what the girl needs. Every guy who wants her for an hour gives her money that ends up in the hands of her pimp. You've got to convince her to get off the street. Next time try a little Christian compassion."

Jude shook his head. "That's not my area of expertise."

Sarah's heart softened. "Look at it this way, Jude, there are rules out here on the street, just like in the military. You could get a girl killed by interfering."

"What about you?" he shot back.

"I get them off the street. Away from this area, the rules change. They're safe at the shelter."

"Until they run back again."

"You got that right." The driver turned and extended his hand to Jude. "Name's Benjamin Ulysses Lejeune. Folks call me Bull."

"Right time, right place. Thanks."

"Brian's a good cop. Just a little quick with the cuffs. Best way to stay out of trouble is to try not to attract attention."

"I'll remember that."

Bull shifted his focus back to the street and turned the key in the ignition. "Where'd you park your car?"

"Next to an all-night doughnut shop, five blocks west of here."

Bull eased the van into the flow of traffic. Picking up his cell off the console, he punched in a number.

"Antwahn, my man. How goes it?" Bull chuckled. "I hear ya. Listen, I need a favor." He paused. "Friend of mine left his wheels in the parking lot across from your place."

Bull glanced back at Jude. "Make? Model?"

"Red Toyota Tundra."

Bull relayed the information. "Got that, Antwahn? My friend would appreciate no misfortune befalling his vehicle until we get over there." Bull chuckled again, this time a low rumble that carried more threat than humor before he slapped the cell shut.

Sarah adjusted her seat belt and glanced out the front window, still mad at herself for sending Jude on a wild-goose chase that could have gotten him in serious trouble.

The captain might be able to handle himself in combat, but life on the street was a different matter. Besides, she'd bet his commanding officer wouldn't have appreciated a call from Atlanta Vice.

Neon lights advertising forbidden pleasure flashed in the night. Sarah blinked at their perverse glare. Up ahead something caught her eye. She crooked her neck as a familiar face came into focus.

Tapping Bull's shoulder, she said, "Isn't that Keesha's friend?"

"Velvet jacket and leather miniskirt? Yeah, that's her."

"Pull over." Sarah slid the panel door open as the van stopped.

The girl on the street turned wary eyes toward Sarah.

"Brittany, you must be hungry, working this late in the cold. We've got food back at Hope House."

The girl shook her head. "Don't you ask me to come back to the house with you, Ms. Sarah."

"I bet you haven't eaten all day."

"Damian's gonna take me out for a steak dinner once I finish up tonight."

"Uh-huh." Sarah stepped onto the sidewalk and walked slowly toward the girl. "Keesha said she misses you."

The girl's face clouded. "Keesha still with you?"

"She's taking classes at Georgia State and earning money by helping out around the house."

"Don't tell her you saw me."

"One night, Brittany. A hot shower. A good meal. A bed of your own. Then you can decide what you want."

The girl's bottom lip quivered. "Damian said he'd kill me next time I go with you."

Sarah pointed to the van. "You know Bull won't let Damian hurt you."

The girl peered around Sarah's shoulder. "Who's the other guy? A cop?"

Sarah turned. "He's a new volunteer."

"Don't look like he belong around here."

Sarah studied Jude for a long moment. "Maybe not. But he's trying."

Jude started to say something. Sarah flashed him a look she hoped he understood. *Keep your mouth shut.*

Wrapping her arm around the girl, Sarah gently ushered her toward the van. "Jude, you move up with Bull."

Without a word of protest, he hopped out of the van.

"Good to see you again, Brittany," Bull said as she and Brittany climbed into the rear.

Jude tugged the panel door shut, then slid into the front passenger seat.

At the next intersection, Bull made a U-turn. "Hope you don't mind, Jude, my man, but I'm gonna take the ladies back to the house. Once Brittany's settled in, I'll drive you to your vehicle."

In the rear, Sarah patted Brittany's arm. "Everything's going to be okay."

Hopefully, her words would prove true.

Sarah sighed, tired of the pain she saw in the eyes of the kids she pulled off the street. She knew all too well the heavy baggage some children had to carry. Brittany had more than her fair share.

Sarah thought of her own life. A mother who ran

through men like water through a sieve. Always searching for love.

Somehow Sarah had never filled those holes, no matter how hard she'd tried. Eventually, she'd realized her mother didn't need her or want her. A hard reality for a child to accept.

And what about the guy sitting in front of her? He'd be on his way soon enough. Having him underfoot reminded her of a promise she'd made to herself.

Never get involved with men.

When the van pulled to a stop behind the three-story brick house on Rosemont Avenue, Jude hopped out and opened the side panel for the women. Sarah held Brittany's arm and ushered her toward the back door, the porch light shining a circle of welcome in the otherwise desolate night.

Jude followed them into the large kitchen. An industrial stove and oversize refrigerator took up the far wall. The center of the room was filled with a large metal table that appeared to double as a workstation. A lower shelf held mixing bowls and baking dishes.

A young African-American girl, early twenties, pretty with high cheekbones and a warm smile, entered the kitchen. "Brittany," she shrieked, throwing her arms around the new arrival.

The two hugged, tears streaming down their cheeks. Sarah rubbed Brittany's back as Keesha jabbered.

"I didn't think I'd ever see you again, girl. Where've you been? On the street? Honey child, there's no reason to be doing that. Ms. Sarah, Bull and everyone here at the shelter, they want to help you."

"Keesha, why don't you take Brittany upstairs to the girls' dorm and get her settled?" Sarah suggested. "Then you two come down to the chapel. There's leftover lasagna in the fridge that I'll stick in the oven so Brittany can eat after night prayer."

The girls continued to chatter as they left the kitchen. Sarah glanced at Jude. "When was your last meal?"

"Breakfast at the mess hall this morning."

"Bet that was tasty."

His lips twitched. "Are you always so feisty?"

"Feisty?"

"That's right. You act like a first sergeant ordering everyone around."

She put her hands on her hips and tried not to smile. Pretty even when she was fussing at someone.

"So tell me, Jude, do first sergeants get to pull rank on captains?"

He couldn't help but laugh. "Why no, ma'am. They work together to get the job done."

She pointed to the refrigerator. "Then grab the lasagna from the fridge while I turn on the oven."

"Maybe I'll have to demote you, ma'am."

"Not a chance." Sarah took the Pyrex dish from his hands and shoved it in the oven. "Should take about thirty minutes to heat up. You're welcome to stay."

"I appreciate the offer, but Bull said he'd drive me back to my truck."

"After night prayer." Bull stepped in from the cold. He slipped out of his jacket and hung it on a peg by the door. "Why don't you join us?"

Jude shook his head. "I really need to get on the road."

"Of course you do." Sarah glanced at the clock on the wall. "But it's almost 10:00 p.m., and you're exhausted. Maybe you should eat something and then go back to your motel."

Jude pursed his lips. "Fact is I never got a room."

"But you changed your clothes?" she said as she arranged plates and silverware on the table.

"In a public restroom. I guess the first thing I need is the closest motel."

Bull snickered. "Jude, my man. Fleabag is not what you want. Why don't you stay here?"

Sarah's head flew up.

Bull held up his hands. "Now, Sarah, you know we've got extra bunks in the boys' dorm, and I could use the help. No telling when that funding will come through for another overnight employee."

He slapped Jude's shoulder. "My advice, we get your truck, then you come back to the shelter. Nothin' good happens on the street this hour of the night."

Keesha peered into the kitchen. "Everyone's in the chapel."

"We'll be right there." Sarah glanced at Jude. "If you want to wash up, the boys' latrine is downstairs."

"Latrine?"

Her eyes sparkled. "Works with the first-sergeant persona."

He followed her out of the kitchen and down a long hallway. Photos of teens lined the walls. Black, white, Asian, Latino, all of them smiling.

Sarah showed him the stairway to the boys' dorm, then pointed down the hall. "The chapel is the third door on the right."

Jude found the latrine, glad to wash the city grime from his hands. Retracing his steps, he stopped at the door Sarah had indicated.

Might as well check out the chapel. Anything—even prayer—would be better than sitting alone in the kitchen.

The sweet scent of candles filled the air as Jude stepped inside the small room. Three roughly hewn, wooden crosses hung on the wall behind a table that held a plant in an earthenware pot. Nearby a large leather-bound Bible lay open on a small stand.

Kids sat on the carpeted floor, heads down, legs crossed. Jude counted eight boys and five girls, who all looked like normal teens.

Sarah flipped on a CD player. A woman sang about forgiveness, redemption and the love of the Lord, repeating the syllables in a soothing cadence.

Jude hunkered down in the rear, away from the kids but with a clear view of Sarah, who clasped her hands, head bowed. Bull entered and took a spot on the opposite side of the room.

"Jesus forgave the sinner…" The plaintive song filled the small room and mixed with the wisps of smoke twisting from the candles.

Jude tilted his head back against the wall. Above him, a heater vent pumped tepid air that brushed his cheek and was as soothing as a woman's touch.

His eyes drooped. He was back in the desert. An IED exploded. He jerked, caught himself. His eyes popped open.

Had anyone seen him doze off? He glanced at Sarah, still bent in prayer.

Did God listen to her?

His eyes flicked over the kids. Did God listen to any of them?

He stared at the two smaller crosses on the wall. Good thief, bad thief.

A story of forgiveness. Or so his father claimed. Ironic, really, but that was the issue, wasn't it?

Would he ever be able to forgive his dad?

Jude shook himself, hoping to shove the thought into the darkness.

But the memory took hold like an obsession.

A stalled car, an oncoming train. They'd all escaped, until Jude's mother ran back to get…

The heart-shaped money clip she'd hung on the visor. The only memento she had from her dad.

So why hadn't *his* father reacted?

A lump clogged Jude's throat.

The sound of screeching metal…his mother's scream…

Jude tried to remember her face. Brown hair. Blue eyes. Tall. Wasn't everyone tall to a six-year-old kid?

A heaviness settled over him. A sorrow for the little boy left behind. For a father whose grief twisted into an inability to relate to his young son. Worse than anything had been the self-righteousness. His dad believed that he walked with the Lord.

To a boy who felt isolated and alone, if his father

walked with the Lord that was the last place Jude wanted to be.

He glanced at Sarah. Was her belief twisted, as well? Did she claim God was all loving when He allowed the sick perversions that forced so many kids to seek shelter from the reality of their lives?

Jude knew what it was like to have to escape. An ROTC scholarship to college had been his way out. He hadn't looked back.

Now, seeing the kids in this room, he realized he'd been one of the lucky ones.

The song faded to silence. Then a small voice spoke. "Father, thank you for taking me from a place of pain and bringing me to a place of safety."

A girl wept. Her sorrow cut through Jude. So young and so hurt.

"Thank you, Lord, for bringing Brittany back to us." Keesha wrapped her arm around the teen with the woman's body and the troubled eyes.

"Thank you for bringing Captain Walker to Hope House." Jude's head flew up at the sound of Sarah's voice. "Help him find his friend."

Evidently, Sarah believed in the power of prayer. Well, she could talk to the Lord all she wanted. Jude would count on his own ability to find Nicole.

He wanted to leave the stuffy room, the house on Rosemont and Sarah Montgomery with her questioning eyes and love of the Lord.

Jude rose and headed for the door. He didn't need to be sucked into the hypocrisy of faith. He'd left all that behind when he turned his back on his father. He would leave it behind once again.

Sarah watched Jude bolt from the chapel. The captain acted like one of the troubled kids they picked up off the street. Jude Walker may be put together on the outside, but he was hurting inside. Was it because of the woman he was trying to find? Or perhaps pain he carried from his past?

She glanced at Bull and nodded.

He rose and slipped from the room.

Maybe Bull could help.

Hopefully, once Jude found Nicole, his girlfriend would be able to smooth out the rough edges of his life.

Funny for a woman to give a man the wrong address. Was she related to Viki Valentine? Although Sarah barely remembered the girl, her history couldn't be good.

So many of the kids were trapped in a self-perpetuating cycle of despair. Hard to climb into the light when you had grown up in darkness.

Sarah thought back to the last man her own mother had brought home. A retired factory worker with a monthly pension and medical benefits. Somehow in her mother's mind that equated to security. Unfortunately, it had nothing to do with love.

Sarah lowered her head and prayed.

*Lord, I'm trying to leave the past and move into the future You have prepared for me. But it's hard to know Your will for my life. If a door opens, give me the courage to walk through it.*

# THREE

After night prayer, Sarah insisted Brittany eat a hefty helping of lasagna before she and Keesha went upstairs to the girls' dorm. Sarah tidied the kitchen but left out a plate and silverware in case Jude wanted something to eat when he returned to the shelter.

If he returned.

Bull had posted a note on the bulletin board, saying he was driving Jude back to his truck.

Big and burly, but with a heart of gold, Bull had a way with people. Sarah smiled.

For all his history, Bull had turned his life around. It was hard to believe that the stories about his youth were true. Supposedly he'd controlled the neighborhood, but not in a good way. When his brother—a dedicated cop who was making a difference—was gunned down, God had walked into the midst of Bull's pain and claimed him as His own.

Maybe Bull could get through to the captain and find out what had sent him racing from the chapel.

Sarah wiped her hands on a dish towel and headed for her office. Dropping into the chair behind her desk, she spotted the blinking answering machine and pushed Play.

"Sarah, it's Mom. I just wanted to hear your voice, sugar."

Sarah bit down on her lip.

"It's been so long since we've talked. I know I've made a lot of mistakes. I thought things would be better when I married Hank. He said to tell you…well, he's trying to be a good stepdad, but he thinks you're running away. Call me, sugar. I'm sure we can—"

"Work things out," Sarah mumbled, punching the delete message button. Isn't that what her mother always tried to do?

Except her idea of problem solving involved bringing a new man home. Her mother didn't understand long-term commitment or self-sacrifice. Nor did she understand her daughter's desire to make her *own* way in the world.

Sarah didn't need a man to complete her. She was fine just the way she was.

"Parents!" she mumbled. Then, realizing she sounded like one of the kids, she laughed out loud.

"You okay?" Keesha stepped into the office.

"I'm fine. What'd you find out about Brittany?"

"Her momma's sister lives in Macon." Keesha handed Sarah a three-by-five card. "Here's the aunt's name and phone number. I told Brittany you'd talk to her tonight."

"How'd she react?"

"I think she's relieved. Her mother has another year in prison before she's up for parole. Evidently she signed all the forms with Family Services for the aunt to take over guardianship. You know Brittany doesn't want anything to do with her dad."

The last time Brittany stayed at the shelter, Sarah had seen her bruises. She would drive Brittany to Macon if need be to ensure the girl wouldn't have to face her abusive father again.

"Thanks, Keesha. I'll be sure to tell Cynthia what a great job you've been doing while she's been gone."

"It'll be nice to have her back, but I don't want to even think about you leaving. Have you heard anything about the orphanage position?"

"The board won't make a decision for a while yet."

"South America." Keesha sighed wistfully. "It sounds so exciting."

"Setting up a program to promote American adoptions of Colombian children?" Sarah laughed. "Sounds like a lot of work to me."

"At least we'll have you with us for a little longer."

Sarah's heart warmed. Keesha was a hardworking young woman who had cleaned up her life. Now she was taking classes toward a degree and helping with the kids.

When Keesha headed back upstairs, Sarah called Brittany's aunt, who agreed to pick her niece up first thing in the morning.

Call completed, Sarah turned her attention back to the financial reports. She added up the funds Hope House had received from the foundation over the last six months, then reviewed the Caring Heart's records for the same time period and checked the contributions.

Why didn't the figures add up?

She rubbed her fingers over her temples, hoping to ease the pressure that had been building since her earlier conversation with Winton, when the sound of a car CD player broke through the stillness outside.

Sarah tugged back the curtain. A gold Eldorado pulled to the curb.

A twinge of apprehension slid down her spine as she grabbed her sweater and stepped into the foyer.

"That's Damian's car," Brittany cried from the top of the landing. Keesha peered over her friend's shoulder.

"Go back into the dorm and close the door, Brittany. Keep the lights off and don't go near the window." Sarah reached for the doorknob. "Keesha, call Bull's cell. Tell him I need him back here now."

Sarah pulled the door open and stepped into the chilly night. The light from the porch scattered over the sidewalk. The Eldorado sat in the shadows beyond, heavy base thumping through the cold.

Wrapping the sweater around her shoulders, Sarah crossed her arms over her chest and stared at the vehicle. Hopefully, her stance would send a signal to keep moving down the street.

The hair on the back of her neck prickled as the driver's door opened. A man she recognized stepped onto the pavement. Tall and slender, he wore a fur coat and flared jeans. A thick silver chain dangled from his pocket.

"What do you want, Damian?" she called out. Luckily, her voice didn't expose the nervousness that fluttered through her stomach.

Damian sauntered toward her, a sneer plastered on his long face. "I came to get Brittany. Take her home with me." He jammed his thumb back at his chest in a possessive motion packed with defiance.

Sarah kept her voice calm. "She doesn't want to be with you anymore, Damian. Now, turn around and get back in your car before I call the police."

"Cops are tied up with a raid downtown. They

won't be comin' this way. Plenty of time for me to go in there and get my woman."

Sarah stepped to the edge of the porch. "It's late, Damian. Go home."

The glint in his eye told her he wasn't about to leave.

Where was Bull?

Damian reached for Sarah's arm. She jerked free and ran for the door.

At that instant a red pickup charged down the street and screeched to a stop.

Footsteps sounded on the sidewalk. Glancing over her shoulder, Sarah saw a whirl of movement.

"Jude?"

He grabbed Damian by the shoulders, spun him around and smashed his fist into the punk's jaw.

Damian crumpled onto the grass.

"Get out of here." Jude's voice was low and dangerous. "And don't come back again."

Damian staggered to his feet, rubbing his chin.

Jude snagged his shirt collar and leaned into his bloodied face. "And if you ever touch her again, I'll make sure it's the last thing you do."

"Son of a—" His hand groped along the waistband of his jeans.

"Watch out," Sarah screamed, seeing the knife he brandished.

In one smooth movement, Jude grabbed Damian's wrist with his left hand and twisted. His right fist jabbed into the punk's gut, causing him to double over and drop the knife to the ground.

Jude pulled him up by the collar and shoved him along the sidewalk. "Don't come back, you understand me?"

Grunting a reply, Damian slithered into the Eldorado.

Bull raced around the corner of the house just as the car disappeared from sight. "Where is that scum bag?"

"Already taken care of." Jude picked up the knife Damian had dropped and quickly explained what had happened.

Bull pulled out his cell. "I'll call the cops and let them know. Damian's caused a lot of problems in the area recently. Word is, he's trying to expand his turf."

Danger past, Sarah slumped with relief. If Jude hadn't arrived when he did—

He was staring at her. She saw concern in his eyes, but when he spoke, his voice was stern.

"Did he hurt you?"

She shook her head. "I…I'm fine. Thanks to you."

The light from the porch caught the set of his square jaw. "Why didn't you stay inside with the door locked?"

"What?"

"You heard me, Sarah. It was foolish to come outside. Did you think you'd scare him away?"

She bristled. As soon as Damian climbed out of his car, she'd realized her mistake. Not that she wanted to admit she'd been wrong. "I was worried about Brittany's safety."

"Yeah, well, locking the door and staying inside would have been a wiser course of action. You put yourself in danger. That's not smart."

She tapped her foot with annoyance, wanting to be anywhere but caught in Jude's reproving glare. She was cold and tired and her emotions were pulled to the breaking point.

Retreat was sometimes the best option.

She did a crisp about-face that would make any first sergeant proud and reached for the doorknob. As she stepped inside, Keesha and Brittany tumbled down the steps followed by the rest of the girls.

"Oh, my goodness. Captain Jude, you're awesome to go up against Damian," Brittany squealed as Jude followed Sarah into the foyer. The boys raced upstairs from their basement dorm room and surrounded him, as well.

Pretty obvious no one was going back to bed anytime soon.

"Hot chocolate and cookies," Bull called over the

confusion as he scooted inside. "Keesha, you're in charge."

The kids ran to the kitchen, leaving the three adults behind.

Bull touched Sarah's shoulder. "Jude's right. You never should have gone outside to confront Damian. I told you before, don't be messing with street scum like him. If he can't find Brittany…"

"I've already called her aunt. Brittany's leaving in the morning," she said.

Bull glanced at Jude.

Sarah looked from one man to the other, tired of defending her actions. She threw her hands up in the air. "I was just trying to protect the kids."

Jude's face softened. "Of course you were. But if Damian hears you've helped Brittany get out of town, next time he won't be looking for Brittany. He'll be looking for you."

She tried to muster a confidence she didn't feel. "Damian doesn't scare me."

Jude tilted his head and raised his brow. "Now who are you trying to fool?"

Her shoulders drooped ever so slightly. "Probably myself. But I won't let him hurt the kids."

"Just make sure he doesn't hurt you, either."

A strand of hair fell over her cheek. Jude reached out and tucked it behind her ear.

His touch sent a shiver down Sarah's spine that

had nothing to do with Damian and had everything to do with the man standing in front of her.

She stepped back. "It's late, Jude, and you still need to find a motel room." Surely he'd take the hint and say good-night.

"Maybe I'd better stick around in case Damian comes back." He nodded to Bull. "You mentioned a bunk in the boys' dorm."

Bull's face broke into a wide grin. "It's got your name on it, my man." He slapped Jude's shoulder. "I sure could use the help. Now, why don't both of us have a plate of lasagna and some of those cookies before the kids eat all of them."

Sarah watched the two men walk toward the kitchen. The way her heart was pounding, she wasn't sure who she should worry about more, Damian or Jude?

# FOUR

Light from the hallway scattered across the wall of the boys' dorm, illuminating the clock in the corner: 0400 hours. Two hours since Jude had crawled into the bunk, yet sleep continued to elude him. Too many questions raced through his mind.

With a sigh he reached into the duffel he'd stashed under the bed, found the photo and raised it into the half-light. Nicole's eyes stared back at him.

Why had she given him this address? Was it because of Viki?

Hopefully, he'd locate the younger Miss Valentine in the morning. Surely she'd have information he could use to track down Nicole. If the two were even related.

Returning the photo to the duffel, his fingers touched another piece of paper. He knew what the message said before he pulled it into the light.

"Don't try to find me."

The e-mail he'd tried to ignore. Could it be part of a silly game Nicole was playing to see if he loved her enough to search for her?

He almost laughed. If she thought he'd back off because of one ridiculous message, she didn't know the kind of guy he really was.

Or had something else happened?

Tomorrow was a new day. God willing, he'd find her.

God? He shook his head. Sarah must be rubbing off on him.

Finding comfort with the thought, he closed his eyes and settled into a restful sleep.

The next morning Jude followed the smell of coffee into the kitchen and found Sarah standing over the stove, scrambling eggs and flipping pancakes.

"There's juice in the fridge. Help yourself to the coffee," she said as he entered. "Cream and sugar's on the counter."

She was dressed in a denim skirt, white blouse and red sweater, looking very patriotic and much too energetic for the amount of sleep she must have had. The kids hadn't gone back to their dorms until late last night.

Now the winter sun was trying to burn through

the haze of a new day. One that he hoped would lead him to Nicole.

Jude dropped his duffel by the back door and glanced at his watch. Still early. He might as well accept Sarah's hospitality for a few more minutes.

He poured a cup of the hot brew and took a sip. "Coffee's just what I needed."

"Everyone's still talking about how you walloped Damian."

"The good guys won. That's what the boys like to hear," Jude said.

"I think what they like is a guy who's willing to talk to them. Bull said the boys kept you up most of the night."

"They wanted to know about the army. I told them, if they were willing to work hard and keep their noses clean, Uncle Sam could use them. Might be a step up from what I saw last night."

Sarah stirred the eggs. "I don't know much about the military except that anyone who served in the Middle East deserves a good breakfast. Cereal and doughnuts are in the dining room where the kids eat. I thought you might like a heartier meal."

She piled the eggs and pancakes onto a plate and held it out to him. "Your breakfast, sir."

Once again he glanced at his watch. "Sarah, I really need to—"

"Look for that girlfriend of yours. I know, but you have to eat."

"Bull said you could be stubborn." Smiling, he accepted the plate, grabbed utensils from a basket on the counter and pulled a tall stool to the work-table. "Thanks for the chow and a place to sleep."

"After what you did…" She shrugged. "Despite what I said last night, I'm very grateful for your help."

Jude raised his fork, laden with egg. "Bull also said you try to take care of everything around here by yourself."

She rolled her eyes, but her lips eased into a smile. "Bull talks too much."

"Did I hear my name?" As if on cue, he pushed through the kitchen door and moaned. "Coffee. I need coffee."

"You should have made the boys settle down so you and Jude could have slept."

"And miss the war stories? No way." Bull winked at Jude. "I told you, man. She loves to throw her weight around."

"It's the first sergeant coming out."

Sarah gave them both a reproving glare as she lined up corrugated boxes on the work counter and started to fill them with staples from the pantry.

Bull took a long swig from his cup and wiped the back of his hand over his mouth.

"Sarah, I've got to check on the kids in the work-study program. Better cancel that outreach today. I don't want you wanderin' the streets alone with Damian on the prowl."

She frowned. "I'm not going to change my plans just because of what happened last night."

Bull looked at Jude. "Say, man, you free for a few hours?"

Jude gulped. "Ah…"

"I'll be fine," Sarah insisted. "The kids have already left for their Saturday jobs, and Brittany's aunt picked her up an hour ago."

Jude shoved the last forkful of eggs into his mouth and placed his utensils on his plate. "Food deliveries?"

"That's right. To some of the folks in the neighborhood." Bull nudged Jude's shoulder.

Sarah shook her head. "I don't need protection, Bull."

"But Jude wants to find Viki Valentine's sister. You can ask about both sisters when you're making your calls. Someone will have information."

Bull slurped down the rest of the coffee. "Besides, if you don't let Jude go with you, he'll be givin' more money to the girls on the street. Doubt the cops would buy that volunteer story two nights in a row."

Sarah reached into the pantry for more cans. "I'm sure Jude can stay out of trouble."

"Accept the man's help, Sarah."

Bull placed his cup in the sink, then, pulling his coat from the wall peg, he spotted Jude's bag on the floor. "Hey, man. The bunk's available for as long as you're in town."

Jude nodded his thanks.

"Forgot to tell you, Sarah. Your mother called when you were in the shower this morning. I gave her your cell number."

Sarah flinched. A can dropped from her hand.

Jude stooped to retrieve it, noticing the tight line around her lips. Evidently, she didn't want her cell number given out to anyone, including her mom.

Oblivious to the effect his comment had on Sarah, Bull waved goodbye and closed the door behind him.

As Sarah filled the last two boxes with bag lunches and bottled water, Jude mulled over his options. Helping with the morning outreach might pay off. Best-case scenario, he'd pick up information about Nicole. Worst case, by noon, he could strike out on his own.

"Bull's right. You shouldn't make deliveries alone," he finally said.

Sarah closed the boxes and turned to look at him,

a stubborn determination evident in the tilt of her head. "I don't need a bodyguard."

"Just let me lend a hand, okay?"

Before she could respond, he grabbed a box off the counter. "Whether you like it or not, I'm yours for the day."

Sarah slid behind the wheel of the shelter's van, grateful Jude had insisted on accompanying her. Sure, she could have made the deliveries on her own, but having him along would make the time pass more quickly.

Plus, she *was* worried about running into Damian. Of course, if Jude asked her point-blank, she would probably deny the truth. No reason for him to think that little episode on the porch last night had shaken her to the core.

Jude was right. Confronting a street thug face-to-face had been a mistake. In fact, she'd tossed and turned all night, thinking about what could have happened. Thank God, Jude had arrived in time.

She glanced at him, sitting in the passenger seat. He wore khaki slacks and a light blue shirt that matched his eyes. Before they left the house, he had pulled a navy Windbreaker from his pack and looked totally nautical as if he was ready for a day at sea instead of patrolling the streets of Atlanta.

Get your mind on the road, she sighed, jamming

the gear into Drive. At the end of the street, Sarah made a right onto Moreland, and four blocks south she turned west into the heart of the area they'd cruised last night.

A few men milled around the parking lot of a beverage store, waiting for the Closed sign to be switched to Open.

"Morning brew must be a little stronger than coffee for that crew," Jude said.

"A sad fact of life around these parts, I'm afraid."

The trill of a cell phone filled the car. Sarah rummaged through her purse until she found the cell, checked caller ID and then tossed it back into her handbag.

Jude raised his brow. "Mama?"

"I'll call her later."

Two blocks west, they pulled into the parking lot behind a cluster of apartments.

Dogs barked in the distance. A curtain moved in one of the windows. Sarah could feel eyes watching them as they stepped from the van.

"Stay cool, okay?"

Jude crooked a brow. "You still upset because I tagged along?"

"You're a stranger around here, Jude. Don't go off on your own."

He raised his hand to his forehead in a mock

salute. "Roger that, ma'am. But I think I can handle myself."

She looked up at him, the glare from the winter sun causing her to squint. "Then do me a favor. Grab some of those boxes from the back so we can make our visits."

"Whatever you say, ma'am."

Boxes in hand, they climbed to the second floor and made three deliveries before heading back downstairs where Sarah knocked on a door at the end of the hall.

"Ms. Hattie, it's Sarah Montgomery from Hope House."

The scuffle of feet filtered into the stairwell. Sarah tilted her head toward the peephole and smiled.

A series of locks unbolted before the door pulled open and a wizened prune of a face peered out. Rheumy eyes stared at Sarah for a long moment, then a large welcoming smile spread across the old woman's face.

"I just been asking the Lord when I was gonna get a visitor." Her brows raised in surprise as she glanced at Jude standing behind Sarah. "He always brings me more than I ask. Now I've got two visitors."

She pulled the door open wide. "Y'all come in. Can you sit a spell? Have a cup of hot tea?"

Sarah stepped inside and beckoned Jude forward. As usual, the tiny apartment was spotless and smelled of lemon cleaner. Hand-crocheted doilies and tatted lace decorated the backs of the over-stuffed furniture, probably vintage 1940s but amazingly well preserved. A small mahogany pedestal table and four chairs gleamed with polish in the dining area where a glass-front hutch held crystal bowls and a teacup collection.

"Ms. Hattie, you know how generous the people are to donate food for the kids. We're overstocked, and I would appreciate if you could take some of the extra off my hands."

Ms. Hattie shook her head. "Waste not, want not." She shuffled toward Jude and peered in the box he carried. "Um-ummm, grits and cornbread. Molasses, black-eyed peas and a canned ham."

Narrowing her eyes, she looked at Sarah. "You sure you can't use all this?"

Sarah didn't want to lie, but Ms. Hattie lived on a fixed income and was a proud woman who would never accept a handout. "This is excess, Ms. Hattie. You'll be doing me a favor."

The old woman smiled. "Why sure. I be happy to help out."

Placing a wrinkled brown hand on Jude's arm, she nudged him toward the kitchen. "Put the box on the table while I fix you a cup of tea."

"Thank you, ma'am, but Sarah has more people to visit. I doubt we have time to stay for tea. Maybe we can come back another day." He placed the box where Ms. Hattie had indicated and helped the woman unpack the contents.

"Ms. Hattie, Jude's looking for a friend," Sarah said. "Did you ever know a family named Valentine?"

"I know Roy Valentine. Saw him 'bout three weeks ago when I was shopping at Handley's Market. Roy stumbled in, smelling like whiskey."

Sarah nodded, hoping to encourage the woman.

"You know Mr. Handley don't tolerate nonsense in his store. Told him to go back to that I-20 underpass where he holes up."

"Have you seen Roy since then?"

"No. But I've been praying for him, asking the Lord to change his heart."

"I'm sure God listens to your prayers, Ms. Hattie," Jude said.

His sincerity touched Sarah. Seemed Jude was turning into a good volunteer after all.

"Why don't I put these items in your cupboard," he said, causing the old woman's smile to grow even wider.

She pointed to a tall cabinet. "Canned goods go in there."

Jude opened the door, then turned to catch

Sarah's eye. "Didn't you say we had another box of supplies to give away?"

Sarah glanced at the cupboard and immediately understood the real reason for Jude's question. A pound of macaroni, two cans of beans and a box of tea bags were the only items on the shelf.

"You're right. Thanks for reminding me, Jude."

"I'll get the box from the van." He started for the door, but Ms. Hattie grabbed his arm.

"Now, you stay here," she fussed. "Keep me company. Makes an old woman feel young again havin' such a handsome man to help her out."

Sarah could have sworn she saw Jude blush. He glanced her way and shrugged sheepishly.

"Stay with Ms. Hattie. I'll run to the van while you two visit." Sarah held her laughter in check until she stepped outside, making a mental note to notify the free-meal program of Ms. Hattie's need.

Pulling her jacket around her shoulders, Sarah scurried to the van and opened the rear hatch. As she reached for the box on the floor, the roar of a car engine and the blare of rap music sounded behind her.

Her neck prickled. Sarah turned. A gold El-dorado pulled to a stop.

"Where's Brittany?" Damian shouted from the car.

Sarah steeled the nervous flutter in her stomach. "She's left town."

"Why you—" He jerked open the car door and in a flash rounded the Eldorado.

Adrenaline surged through Sarah's veins. She slammed the hatch and ran for the apartment complex. Her heart pounded against her chest.

Glancing over her shoulder to ensure Damian wasn't behind her, Sarah collided head-on with Jude as he charged around the corner.

His eyes were ablaze, hands raised, ready to do battle. "I saw the Eldorado from Ms. Hattie's window. Did he hurt you?"

Sarah shook her head and tried to catch her breath.

Tires squealed.

Jude lunged forward as the Eldorado raced out of the apartment complex. He glared at the disappearing auto and remained at the curb for a long moment before he turned and walked back to where Sarah stood.

She leaned against the stucco wall of the apartment complex, hoping to calm her racing heart.

Jude took the box from her hands and wrapped his arm around her shoulder, pulling her close.

"Are you okay?"

"I…I'm fine," she managed to stammer, resting her head on his shoulder. She closed her eyes, feeling a warmth rush over her.

*What are you doing?*

Her eyes flew open, and she stepped away, hoping her voice wouldn't betray the tangle of emotions that were pinging through her heart.

"We'd better go back inside," she insisted. "Ms. Hattie will wonder what happened to us."

"Once we give her the food, I'll drive you back to the shelter."

"That's ridiculous, Jude. I've got water and bag lunches ready for the men who live under the freeway. Bull and I visit them the third Saturday of every month. They're expecting us."

"But, Sarah—"

"No *buts*. Ms. Hattie said Roy Valentine's living there now. If you're lucky, you'll get the information you need to find Nicole."

"The information can wait."

"If I run back to the shelter, that means Damian's won. I won't let that happen."

Jude hesitated for a second and then nodded. "This time I won't let you out of my sight."

Standing next to Jude, Sarah's pulse continued to race. He was a great guy who deserved to find Nicole.

And what about Sarah? She had closed her heart a long time ago.

Traffic picked up as the van cruised along I-20. Jude insisted on driving while Sarah gave him directions from the passenger seat, still visibly shaken, but trying to be strong.

As he exited the highway, she motioned for him to pull off the road onto a dirt path. A number of large green trash bags lay scattered in the shelter provided by the overhanging ramp.

Jude turned on the hazard lights and cut the engine. "Sure you're up to this?"

"Of course."

Grabbing two of the boxes, he and Sarah approached the protected area. Heads popped up from behind garbage bags Jude realized contained gear and belongings. The men turned to stare at them.

"Stay upwind," Sarah advised.

The weathered faces regarded them with emotionless stares.

Sarah began to distribute the water and lunches, talking to the men, asking about any special needs they might have. Jude hovered close until she pulled him aside.

"You've got to give me a little space."

He glanced at the men. "Remember, I signed on as bodyguard."

"At least be a little more discreet."

Okay, if that's what she wanted, he'd back off a bit. Jude approached a man, midthirties who appeared strong, able to work. What was his story?

Jude gave the guy two bottles of water and a bag lunch, all the while keeping Sarah in sight.

"God bless you," the guy mumbled, his eyes gleaming with gratitude.

Sarah threw Jude an encouraging smile as she walked past him to the van and returned with a first-aid kit, antibiotic ointment and two pairs of socks. Next time he glanced her way, she was pulling off some guy's work boots.

So much for staying upwind.

Sarah slipped on latex gloves and applied a heavy layer of ointment to the guy's blistered feet.

The woman had guts, no doubt about it.

She moved on to another man. From the attention she was giving each of them, you'd think they were old friends.

Oh, yeah, Sarah was legit about her concern for the downtrodden.

She pointed to a man sleeping about twenty feet from the others.

As Jude neared, she lowered her voice. "One of the guys said that's Roy Valentine. Somehow his panhandling landed him enough cash for a pint of whiskey. He staggered in here last night, drank himself to sleep and hasn't moved since. Let's hope the binge didn't finish him off."

Kneeling, Sarah touched the man's arm and gave

him a gentle shake. "Roy, open your eyes. It's Sarah Montgomery. I'm from Hope House."

A heavy stubble of beard darkened his wrinkled face. He sputtered, and his eyes opened into two small slits. He raised his head, attempting to sit. Gravity pulled him back to earth.

Jude hitched an arm around the man's shoulder and raised him to a sitting position. "Come on, buddy."

Roy rubbed his fingers over his forehead, exposing a palm encrusted with blood.

Gently Sarah took his hand and washed the scraped flesh with bottled water, then patted it dry and applied the ointment Jude handed her from the first-aid kit.

Pulling Nicole's photo from his pocket, Jude held it close for Roy to see. "Do you recognize this woman?"

The man grimaced. "Nicole's too good to help her brother. All I wanted was a little money."

So Nicole and Roy were related.

Before Jude could continue, Sarah placed a bag lunch and water on the ground next to his makeshift pallet. "I'll call your family and let them know you're okay."

Jude shot her a frustrated glance. Why change the subject now?

"My grandma lives on Butler Street. Green house two doors down from Diamond Pawn."

"What about Nicole?" Jude pressed. "Do you have any idea where I can find her? Or Viki?"

"Viki's the one in trouble." Roy closed his eyes.

Sarah flicked a worried glance at Jude, who gave the drunk a firm shake. "Why's Viki in trouble?"

"Ra-Rashad."

"Rashad Sway?" Sarah asked. "Is Viki working for him?"

"You see Viki, tell her Roy said to get away from Rashad." Roy snuggled back onto his ragged bedding.

"Tell me about Nicole?" Jude insisted.

Roy's eyes fluttered closed. "She's gone."

"Gone where?" Jude nudged his shoulder.

The guy groaned, then began to snore. Repeatedly Jude tried to rouse him, until Sarah finally touched Jude's arm.

"It's no use. He's not going to wake up."

Jude sighed with frustration. What did Roy mean by saying Nicole was gone? Surely Viki would be more forthcoming about her sister's whereabouts, but the younger sibling seemed as hard to find as Nicole. If he couldn't find Viki, then—

Jude gave Roy one last nudge before he stood and turned to Sarah. "How do I find Rashad?"

She shook her head. "Roy's right. You don't want to get involved with him."

"Because—"

"You name it. Drugs, prostitution, gambling. He runs most of the girls in this area and has his hands on anything illegal."

"Then I'll go to the police."

"And tell them what? That a homeless drunk's worried about his sister? Sorry, Jude, they're not interested."

"In that case, let's find Roy's grandmother. You can tell her you saw her grandson and give her that last box of food. Surely, she'll know how to find Nicole."

Out of habit, Jude touched his pocket, feeling the photo near his heart.

Sarah let out an exasperated breath. Grabbing the first-aid kit, she headed for the van.

Jude watched her walk away. What was Sarah's problem? Maybe she was as frustrated as he felt right now.

Roy's words about Nicole rumbled through his mind.

She's gone...but where?

# FIVE

A nice home, Jude thought as he and Sarah walked toward the front door of the green house down the block from Diamond Pawn. Uncluttered lawn, a whitewashed porch with a glider swing big enough for two.

Sarah knocked on the door while Jude placed the box of food items on the glider.

"Hello," she called out, giving her name.

Seemed everyone in Atlanta was fearful of strangers. Didn't bode well for community outreach.

The door inched open, revealing a tall woman who held a wiggling toddler in her arms.

Jude sucked in a deep breath. The resemblance caught him off guard. Nicole's eyes, high forehead, full lips, but instead of playfulness in the older woman's eyes, he saw apprehension and concern.

"Yes?" She shifted the toddler to her hip. The little boy had curly hair and light brown skin.

"I'm Sarah Montgomery, and this is Jude Walker."

Jude nodded. "Pleased to meet you, ma'am."

"We delivered food to some folks this morning and met your grandson."

The woman's hand went to her throat as surprise slammed across her face. "You saw Roy?"

"Yes, ma'am." Jude glanced at Sarah before he continued. "We ran into him near the interstate. He said to let you know he's doing okay."

"Thank the Lord. That's so good to hear." She pushed the door open. "You folks come on in, please. I'm Opal, and this is Shawn."

Jude smiled at the baby.

The house was neat and clean. A flowered couch and matching love seat sat on an oval braided rug in the cozy living room.

The grandmother placed the toddler on the rug and smiled as he scurried after a ball.

Following the child into the dining room, Jude stopped beside a buffet covered with framed photographs. He recognized a younger Nicole in a cap and gown. Probably high school graduation. Her eyes sparkled back at him.

Another photo included a preteen. Viki perhaps? Arms entwined, the two girls laughed at the camera.

A third photo showed an older boy. Jude leaned down to study the wide eyes and youthful face. Could that be Roy?

"Pictures of my grandchildren, Mr. Walker." Opal's voice pulled Jude back to the living room.

"Nice family, ma'am." He smiled, hoping to cover the pinpricks of anxiety he'd felt over the past five weeks. "I met Nicole on R&R six months ago when I was in Atlanta. Do you know where she's living now?"

Opal gave him a long, hard look. Was she sizing him up, questioning Nicole's taste in men?

"You appear to be a good person, Mr. Walker. I can see why my granddaughter would like you."

Sarah stared at him, as well. He felt awkward under the two women's perusal. The toddler grabbed his leg, and Jude pulled him into his arms, happy to have something else to occupy his attention.

"Nicole had a nice place in the Highlands, was doing well for herself. Then—" Opal shrugged and her face tightened with worry "—she moved out and didn't tell me where she was going."

"You haven't heard from her since?" Sarah asked.

Opal shook her head. "Nicole used to call me every week, but her phone was disconnected about a month ago."

Jude knew that all too well. He'd tried her number so many times from the Middle East, wondering what had happened. "Does she have another listing? Maybe a cell?"

"Not that I know of." Opal opened a drawer on the end table and sorted through a stack of letters. "She sent me money each month. Here's the last note I received about six weeks ago. Her return is on the envelope."

Sarah copied the address onto a piece of paper and handed it to Jude. "Do you have any idea where she could be?"

"Wish I did. Three weeks ago I took a bus to her apartment while a neighbor lady watched Shawn. The outer door to the building was locked so I waited on the sidewalk until a lady came home from work. She told me Nicole had moved out and no one knew where she went."

"What about Viki?" Sarah asked.

Opal's face paled. "That no-good Rashad Sway filled her with drugs so she doesn't know what's important anymore." The grandmother looked at Shawn cuddled in Jude's arms. "You think she'd remember her baby boy."

Viki's child. Jude hated the sense of relief that swept over him. He'd worried that the baby could be Nicole's.

Sarah patted Opal's hand. "I have information at

Hope House about where you can get assistance, since you're raising Shawn on your own. Let me write down the number."

Opal took the scrap of paper Sarah offered. "Thank you."

"We brought food," Jude whispered, realizing Shawn had fallen asleep in his arms. He placed the baby in Opal's lap.

She rewarded him with a broad smile when he fetched the box from the porch. "I appreciate the help."

As they left the house, sadness tugged at Jude's heart. He'd been in combat. Seen death and destruction. But this was a different kind of battle.

Sarah touched his arm. "Are you okay?"

No, he wasn't okay. He was overcome by the despair that swirled through Nicole's family. A homeless brother and a sister addicted to drugs? Had the reality of their lives been too much for Nicole so she'd walked away, distancing herself from the darkness? Is that why Jude couldn't find her?

He wouldn't tell Sarah what he was really thinking, so he shrugged. "Yeah, sure, I'm fine."

Jude looked back at the green house, then down at the Highlands address he held in his hand.

More than ever, he needed to find Nicole. For his own sake? Or Opal's?

Right now, he wasn't sure.

\* \* \*

"There's Nicole's apartment complex." Sarah pointed to a fashionable, three-story brick building with white shutters.

Jude eased the van to the curb. Sarah followed him up the walk and watched as he ran his finger down a list of names etched on a brass plate, hanging by the door. The space next to 3A—Nicole's apartment—was blank. He pushed the buzzer.

"May I help you?" A female voice came over the intercom.

Jude leaned toward the speaker grid. "I'm looking for Nicole Valentine."

"She moved out about three, maybe four weeks ago."

Sarah touched Jude's arm. "Let me handle this."

He stepped aside, and Sarah approached the intercom. "My name's Sarah Montgomery, and I'm the director of Hope House. We're trying to locate Nicole's sister. Perhaps the neighbors have information about the girl."

"Everyone's at work," came the reply. "But if you're from Hope House—"

The door buzzed open. They rode the elevator to the third floor where a woman, wearing khaki slacks and a white shirt, answered the door to apartment 3A and motioned Jude and Sarah inside.

Sarah's eyes swept over the L-shaped living room decorated with Danish furniture in shades of brown. A leather couch and love seat filled the center of the spacious area flanked by two chairs covered in leopard-skin print. A glass-top coffee table sat between the couches and held a stack of books and two thick black candles. Track lighting spotlighted the modern art clustered on the walls.

Upscale and pricey. Nicole must have a high-paying job to afford a furnished place like this.

"What'd you say Nicole did for a living?" Sarah whispered to Jude.

He shook his head, confusion lining his face. "She said she worked in the service industry."

Seemed he was as surprised by the accommodations as Sarah was.

Behind them the door closed and the woman stepped forward.

Jude held out his hand. "I'm Jude Walker and this is Sarah Montgomery."

"My name's Tonya. I'm with the apartment cleaning service." She returned the handshake, then glanced at Sarah. "You run the shelter on Rosemont?"

"That's right."

"My niece ran away about a year ago and ended up there." Tonya rolled her eyes. "You know kids. They never believe their parents are looking out for their best interests. The guy who called, Ben, Bob—"

"Probably Bull."

"He gave my sister tips on how to build a relationship with her daughter. The child's been good as gold ever since."

"I'm glad it worked out." Sarah smiled. "Tonya, do you know if Nicole gave a forwarding address?"

"You'll have to check with Prime Rental. They manage this property."

"Perhaps she left something behind that might help us know where she moved."

"Only thing I found was a trinket tucked between the cushions of the couch. Some type of commemorative coin with an eagle on one side."

"The Screaming Eagle. That's the insignia for the 101st Airborne. My division," Jude said.

Tonya walked into the living room and returned holding the coin. She dropped it into Jude's outstretched hand.

"Something you gave Nicole?" Sarah asked.

"Yeah, but—" He looked at Tonya. "Did you happen to find a money clip in the shape of a heart? It has a tiny cross on the upper left quadrant."

"No, sir. The coin's all I found."

Tonya hesitated for a moment before she turned to Sarah. "I don't want to pry, but doesn't Mr. Cunningham have something to do with Hope House?"

"That's right. Winton Cunningham started the shelter, and his Caring Heart Foundation supports the work we do. Why?"

"He might know about Miss Valentine, seeing how he visited her on a regular basis."

Jude slipped the coin into his pocket. "What do you mean by 'a regular basis'?"

She held her hands up, palms out. "Look, I probably said more than I should have."

Jude glanced from the cleaning lady to Sarah and back to Tonya again. "Is there something I'm not getting?"

"Tonya, Mr. Cunningham's married," Sarah said, hoping to end a conversation that seemed to be headed in the wrong direction.

"Yes, ma'am. His wife's a real pretty lady, from what I hear, but…well, I don't want to be spreading gossip, but he came here a lot."

"They were probably working on a project together," Sarah offered. At least that's what she hoped they were working on.

"I'm sure they were," Tonya said, although her tone of voice was less than convincing. "You folks can look around the apartment all you want, but I best be getting back to work."

Sarah and Jude walked through the rooms, but finding nothing that would lead them to Nicole, they thanked Tonya and left the building.

"Mr. Cunningham's well-known for his philanthropic endeavors," Sarah said, hoping to reassure Jude once they were outside. "He and his foundation have helped countless people in need."

"Nicole didn't need help, Sarah."

Hearing the sharp tone in his voice, she wondered if the housekeeper's comments had given him pause.

Jude was like other men she'd known. They wanted everything wrapped up nice and neat. But women were sometimes hard to read.

"Jude, you can't know everything about a woman just because you shared a hotel room for a couple weeks."

"Shared a room?" He raised his brow. "Where'd you get that idea?"

"Well, I...I just presumed."

"You presumed wrong. Nicole and I met at a coffee shop the second day I was in town. Yes, we were staying at the same hotel. Strange as it may sound, she said she liked to take vacations without having to travel out of town. But she had her room, and I had mine. Is that understood?"

"Yes. Of course. But when you said you'd gotten together over your R&R, I thought—"

"Apology accepted. Now, let's go see Winton Cunningham and find out what he can tell us about Nicole."

"You'll have to wait until Monday. Unless—"

"Unless what?"

Sarah looked into Jude's blue eyes and suddenly wanted to wipe away the confusion she'd seen since he first knocked on the shelter's door. He had so many questions about Nicole that remained unanswered. Maybe Winton could provide some information.

"He'll be at the Drake Hotel tonight for a charity ball. I have to accept a check for Hope House and planned to go alone."

The corners of Jude's mouth edged upward. "Why, Ms. Montgomery, I'd be honored to be your escort. Black tie, I presume."

"Yes, but—"

"I've got my dress blue uniform in the truck, okay? What time shall I be ready?"

Seeing Jude's enthusiasm, she suddenly wondered if going together was a good idea. Jude Walker was smitten by a woman he'd met six months ago. No reason for Sarah to get attached to a guy who had feelings for someone else.

"We'll leave the house at six," she said, realizing there was no way she could back out now.

"Then it's a date."

# SIX

Sarah stood in front of the floor-length mirror and stared at her reflection. The dress fit as though it had been made for her. Totally extravagant, but so beautiful.

Ever since she returned to the shelter, she'd had a hard time focusing on anything. Jude Walker's face kept floating through her thoughts, leaving her frustrated and irritable. Why had she invited him to the ball?

She shook her head. Actually, she hadn't invited him. She'd merely mentioned Winton and the Drake Hotel, and somehow Jude had jumped to the conclusion she was looking for a date.

Sure, she could have set him straight, yet it would be nice to have an escort for such a grand affair.

Before Jude had dropped into her life, she had planned to arrive at the hotel shortly before the presentation and leave as soon as she received the check.

Black tie?

She didn't own a ball gown. A long skirt and silk blouse would have been acceptable had she been going alone. But when Sarah told Keesha about the date, the dear girl had called Patrice, who owned a boutique of slightly used fashions donated by Atlanta's rich and famous.

Who would believe Patrice would personally deliver a floor-length gown with a taffeta underskirt and yards and yards of flowing chiffon in a shade of green that made Sarah's eyes sparkle? Or so Patrice and Keesha both said when they slipped the gown over Sarah's head.

"Reminds me of Cinderella going to the ball to meet her Prince Charming," Keesha whispered as she and Patrice left minutes ago.

Sarah waved her hand in the air, hoping to send thoughts of Prince Charming scurrying into la-la land. No need to build more into the evening than a chance for Jude to find out what Winton Cunningham knew about Nicole. Besides, the way Jude kept tapping his shirt pocket where he kept her picture, the captain had only one woman on his mind.

But why would Nicole give Jude the wrong address and then skip town? It didn't make sense.

Getting involved on her part didn't make sense, either.

"Jude's waiting for you," Keesha called up the stairs.

Sarah's heart fluttered as she gathered the chiffon skirt in her hands and raced down the stairs. At the bottom landing, she came to an abrupt halt.

Jude was standing tall and handsome in the foyer, wearing his dress blue uniform, starched white shirt and black bow tie. Rows of medals gleamed on his chest.

He did look like Prince Charming.

Jude turned and stared at her for a long moment. Something flickered in his eyes, and she didn't know if she could breathe.

"Good evening, Sarah."

"Jude."

Why were they being so formal?

He handed her a white rose. "A flower for a beautiful woman."

"You look very nice yourself," she managed to stammer, reaching for the velvet stole—another item from Patrice's boutique—that hung on the coat rack.

"Allow me." Jude took the lush fabric from her hands and wrapped it around her shoulders, his arms enfolding her for a split second in their warm embrace. Stepping to her side, he extended his arm and ushered her toward the door.

Out of the corner of her eye, Sarah spied Keesha

peeking around the kitchen door, a wide grin stretched across her sweet face.

Behind her, Bull waved. "Don't you worry about anything tonight, Sarah. Bull's got it all under control. Now, Keesha, you call the kids for dinner."

Keesha waved. "You two have fun. And be home by midnight."

So like Cinderella's godmother! Sarah laughed as she walked out the door on Jude's arm. Everyone deserved a fairy-tale night, and Sarah planned to make this one last a lifetime.

Jude tucked Sarah into the passenger side of his pickup and slid behind the wheel, wishing he could offer her more fitting transportation to the ball. A truck hardly seemed suitable for the elegant woman sitting next to him.

Sure, he'd recognized Sarah's inner beauty when she'd reached out to Brittany last night on the street corner and again today when they'd delivered groceries to those in need. But he hadn't realized the take-your-breath-away outward beauty Sarah possessed until she'd glided down the staircase, wearing that pretty dress.

He stole a glance at her sitting ramrod straight, hands folded in her lap. Sarah seemed totally oblivious to her beauty or the effect she was having on him. Turning his eyes back to the road, he tried to concentrate on his driving. For a change, Sarah was short on words, which suited him fine. For some reason he felt as tongue-tied as a thirteen-year-old.

Surely his reticence had more to do with the events that had unfolded throughout the day than the woman sitting next to him.

Why had Nicole given him the address for the shelter when she lived in an upscale apartment in the Highlands? Was there something she was trying to hide? Like a dysfunctional homelife? Jude knew about families that weren't always as they seemed.

The fact that Nicole had overcome the obstacles that had pulled her siblings down was something to celebrate, not hide. Hopefully the mystery surrounding her disappearance would be solved once he talked to Winton Cunningham.

Luckily, traffic was light. When Jude and Sarah arrived at the hotel, Jude pulled into valet parking, flipped his keys to the attendant and escorted Sarah into the posh hotel. He couldn't help but note the thick Oriental carpet covering the marble floor and crystal chandeliers glittering from the vaulted ceilings.

"The ballroom's upstairs," Sarah said. They took the elevator to the second floor and were welcomed by the big-band sound of the forties.

A man, probably midfifties, stood at the door to the ballroom, greeting the guests. Medium height and build, brown hair peppered with silver and a smile that seemed less than sincere, he stretched out his arms to Sarah.

Jude stood back, watching the two embrace.

Silk tux. Patent shoes. Fourteen-carat-gold cuff links and studs. No doubt, the illustrious Winton Cunningham.

Sarah laughed at something he whispered in her ear, then pulled back and reached for Jude's arm. "And I want you to meet our newest volunteer at the shelter. Captain Jude Walker, United States Army, and just back from thirteen months in the Middle East."

Jude extended his hand.

"Winton Cunningham," Sarah said, finishing the introductions.

"Pleased to meet you, sir."

"A captain, eh?" His tone of voice made Jude wonder if the rich do-gooder had much regard for those who defended their country.

"We're proud of what Sarah's done at Hope House and the improvements she's made in the last six months."

"Now, Mr. Cunningham, you're embarrassing me."

"I've told you before, Sarah. At social events, call me Winton."

The host flicked an arrogant glance at Jude.

"Sir, I'd like to talk to you about…"

Sarah nudged Jude's arm. "Winton will have a little more time later in the evening."

As much as Jude wanted to question the wealthy philanthropist about Nicole, Sarah was right. With the other guests milling around the entrance, this wasn't the time. Hopefully, a more private opportunity would present itself later in the evening.

Jude placed his hand on the small of Sarah's back. "If you'll excuse us, Mr. Cunningham, you have guests to greet and we need to find our seats."

"Enjoy the evening," Winton said before turning his attention to the next couple in line.

"You like that guy?" Jude said as he and Sarah moved into the ballroom.

The look she shot him made him regret he'd said anything out loud. No reason for Sarah to disparage the hand that funded the shelter.

Jude would have to bite his tongue and squelch the irritation that pricked his neck.

Then he looked at Sarah, standing next to him. Winton Cunningham might be pompous, but Jude could put up with him for one night if he had the opportunity to get to know Sarah a little better. She was a generous woman who cared so much for others.

Did that change the way he felt about Nicole?

An elderly couple shook hands with Sarah, who

turned to include Jude in the conversation. Just that fast he realized nothing was black-and-white.

Sarah made her way through the crowd of well-wishers, thanking them for their donations and answering their questions. Cynthia had told her about the generosity of the people, but Sarah was touched by their interest in the kids and their willingness to help.

When Jude went to the bar, she convinced a technology executive to donate computers to Hope House and provide after-school instruction in basic office skills that would put the kids in good stead for entry-level jobs.

More than she'd ever hoped.

Jude appeared carrying two colas as Mr. Cunningham's beautiful Colombian wife strolled toward them.

Sarah held out her hand. "Elena, it's so nice to see you again. Thank you for inviting me this evening."

"We are happy to have you here, Sarah. You know without Hope House, the Charity Ball would have no reason to occur."

Tall, regal and looking far younger than her fifty-some years, Elena smiled at Jude. "And you have brought a handsome man to add interest to the evening."

Sarah introduced them and watched as the two chatted about South America. Jude seemed able to find common ground with everyone.

"Winton tells me you will be considered for the orphanage position," Elena said, turning back to Sarah. "It's a wonderful opportunity for one lucky person, yes? To take Spanish classes in San Antonio will speed the learning process for the person chosen. My niece recently moved to Atlanta and wished she could have had such a course before she came to the United States."

"I'm sure the class will be a great help to the person selected for the job," Sarah agreed.

"Winton said the decision would be announced soon."

Elena looked at her husband, who was nearby talking to an attractive young woman. "Winton?"

He glanced at his wife. "Yes, my love?"

"Didn't you say that you'd have information soon about the orphanage selection?"

He smiled at Sarah. "A chance to do God's will, as you wrote in your cover letter. I received your application in the mail this afternoon."

"Mr. Cunningham, I'm not sure—"

"Now, Sarah, you understand the preselection contract you signed as part of the paperwork legally binds you to accept the position should you be chosen. Although, I believe I made it perfectly clear

Hope House employees receive no preferential treatment in the selection process."

"Of course, sir. But I've been thinking it might be better if I remain in Atlanta and help Cynthia for the next few months. That way I could ensure the financial situation is ironed out before I—"

"I do not understand." Elena glanced at her husband. "You have found a problem, Winton?"

He took his wife's arm and patted it reassuringly. "Certainly not, dear. Sarah was just a bit confused about how the donations were distributed. Isn't that right?" He looked pointedly at Sarah.

"Why, ah, yes. I—"

"The bookkeeping glitch has been taken care of." Winton cut her off. His lips turned upward, but his eyes were cold. "Now, if you'll excuse us, Elena and I need to take our seats."

Sarah thought back to when she'd signed the application. The end of her six months at Hope House had been quickly approaching. Cynthia's return meant Sarah needed a job. The orphanage position would allow her to move on with her life, which was exactly what Sarah wanted to do.

Or so she had thought.

Winton's comment about shelter employees not receiving preferential treatment played through her mind. Perhaps he'd been letting her know she wouldn't be selected for the position.

A sense of relief swept over her. She could remain in Atlanta a little longer. That would give her time to help Cynthia and ensure Hope House was in the black. Maybe she'd see Jude reunited with Nicole, as well.

In Sarah's opinion the woman was a fool. If and when she met Nicole, Sarah would tell her a few things about the great guy she had left behind.

Once the coffee and dessert were served, Winton Cunningham moved to the podium and tapped on the microphone. The audience quieted and looked expectantly toward the speaker.

"Ladies and gentlemen," he began. "It's my pleasure to welcome you to the Sixth Annual Charity Ball to benefit Hope House. Because of your generosity and the generosity of all the sponsors, the Caring Heart Foundation is able to continue the work done at the shelter. Your donations will benefit the young people throughout the upcoming year with counseling service, medical and dental needs and tutoring and referral services, in addition to maintaining the house and grounds."

Applause sounded in the large ballroom.

"And now, I'd like to introduce Hope House's acting director. Ms. Sarah Montgomery."

Jude stood and held her chair.

"Thank you," she whispered, stepping toward the podium.

"That's some lady," one of the men sitting at the table said when Jude once again took his seat.

He had to agree. Poised and gracious whether working with the homeless or the wealthy.

From what Elena Cunningham had said, Sarah was considering a job in Colombia. Certainly if she could navigate the ins and outs of street life in Atlanta, she could survive—even thrive—anywhere in the world.

The orphanage position would be a wonderful opportunity, but Jude hated to think of Sarah leaving the kids she loved. Maybe he was being selfish, but he'd miss her, as well. Other than Nicole, who was currently MIA, Sarah was the only other woman he knew in the area. Her optimistic disposition must have been infectious because he was confident once he talked to Winton, he'd know how to find Nicole.

As Sarah approached the podium, Winton handed her the check and kissed her cheek. Jude flicked a glance at Elena, who wore a thin, strained smile.

Sarah spoke clearly into the microphone. "On behalf of Hope House, thank you so much for your generosity. The work at the shelter will be able to continue because of your donations."

Jude stood when she returned to the table, her cheeks flushed as she slipped into the seat next to him.

"Good job," he whispered in her ear.

She smiled warmly. "Thanks, Jude. But I'm just a small part of the operation. Cynthia, Bull, even Keesha, they've all done so much."

"I've seen who holds everything together," Jude said, returning her smile.

The band began to play a slow waltz. Winton headed for an attractive woman, early thirties. He offered her his hand and guided her to the dance floor.

"Looks like Mr. Cunningham favors younger women," Jude said softly so only Sarah could hear.

"That woman owns a gift boutique chain and is one of the largest contributors to the foundation."

"Doesn't hurt that she's young and beautiful."

"For goodness' sake, Elena's sitting at the next table."

Jude glanced at Winton's wife, who didn't look happy about the woman on her husband's arm.

When the music ended, Sarah and a number of the other ladies excused themselves to powder their noses. Winton escorted his dance partner back to her seat, then stopped briefly to speak to his wife before he walked out of the ballroom.

Probably a good time to have a little chat with the host. Jude excused himself and headed for the door.

In the hallway Jude spied Winton engaged in

what appeared to be a heated conversation with two men Jude had seen earlier near the bar. As soon as the men headed for the elevator, Jude stepped forward.

"Mr. Cunningham, I wonder if I might have a word with you?"

Winton turned, surprise written on his face. "Captain Walker, isn't it?"

"That's right. I need your help, sir. A friend of mine moved unexpectedly. I'm trying to find her."

"I don't know how—"

Jude pulled Nicole's photo from his pocket and held it up. "You know this woman, don't you, sir?"

Winton's eyes narrowed. He glanced around as if to ensure no one was close enough to overhear.

"I have no idea what you're talking about." Winton's voice was cold and filled with accusation.

Why was he lying?

Jude stepped closer. "I'm talking about Nicole Valentine, sir. Someone told me you visited her often."

"Absolutely not. I've never seen that woman before."

Jude held up the photo again. "Are you sure?"

Winton bristled. "Of course I'm sure. Where do you get off talking to me like that?"

"Because I know you were a frequent guest at her Highlands apartment." Jude held Winton's gaze.

Sweat broke out on Winton's forehead. "Look, if you're trying to blackmail me, it won't work."

Blackmail? Where had that come from?

"Stay away from me, Captain, for your own good."

Jude stared at Winton as he walked back into the midst of the festivities. The only reason Winton would mention blackmail was if he had something to hide.

Jude was relieved to see Sarah had returned to the table when he entered the ballroom. Out of the corner of his eye, he saw Winton whisper into Elena's ear, then step toward the podium.

Winton tapped the microphone. "Ladies and gentlemen, if I may have your attention for a surprise announcement."

The room quieted.

"I've just conferred with the other members of the board. We have decided to award the orphanage position ahead of schedule. A slot opened earlier than expected for the accelerated Spanish course in San Antonio, and we want the new orphanage liaison to have the opportunity to begin classes immediately. I'll be in my office tomorrow, making the final arrangements, so the person selected can leave by the end of the week." Winton held up his hands as a wave of excitement rippled through the audience.

"It is my honor and privilege to announce the person who will spearhead the Colombian orphanage project. A person who has already made a difference in the lives of so many young people in Atlanta."

Winton's eyes flicked over the ballroom, then stopped to glare at Jude. "The new director of the project in Colombia is Sarah Montgomery."

# SEVEN

Jude climbed into his bunk that night, trying to put pieces of a puzzle together that didn't fit. Why had Winton denied knowing Nicole? Had they been involved?

As much as Jude disliked the rich philanthropist, he wanted to give him the benefit of the doubt. But the guy had tipped his hand when he'd made the blackmail comment. Something was going on and it wasn't legit.

Money and power could be bad influences; although, he never thought Nicole was the type of woman who would be swayed by either. Yet he'd known so little about the real Nicole.

Sarah was an enigma, as well.

The atmosphere in the car on the way home from the ball had been tense. Jude hadn't helped the situation with his comments about Winton's wandering eye for younger women, but even when he turned the conversation to Sarah's selection for the orphanage position, she'd remained withdrawn.

Jude had expected exuberance. Instead she appeared pensive and conflicted and even admitted the announcement had taken her by surprise.

He could understand having reservations about leaving Atlanta. But he didn't understand her shortsightedness when it came to Winton Cunningham. She insisted her boss was aboveboard with all his relationships, both business and social.

Of course, Sarah hadn't witnessed the sweat break out on the wealthy tycoon's brow when Jude had questioned him about Nicole. Nor had she heard the anxiety that edged his voice when he'd uttered the blackmail comment.

In Jude's mind that sent up a red flag.

Something Sarah refused to see.

Jude shoved his fist into his pillow. He needed a few hours of shut-eye, but his mind continued to race between thoughts of Sarah in her ball gown and the Nicole he remembered from R&R. Two women, both so different.

Sarah seemed as open as a book. And Nicole?

Visions of her upscale apartment flashed through his mind, the apartment Nicole had kept from him. Why had she given him the address for the shelter when she lived someplace else?

Looking back over the last six months, he wondered about a lot of things.

Finally Jude pulled himself up to a sitting position and dropped his head into his hands. If only he could put it all together, surely—

A board creaked overhead.

The hair on his neck prickled. One of the kids raiding the fridge for a middle-of-the-night snack? Probably, but he might as well check it out to be sure.

Quietly he padded across the floor and pulled open the door to the hallway. The hall light was out and darkness greeted him, along with another moan from the floorboards above.

Doubtful the kids would be walking around in the dark.

Taking the stairs two at a time, he climbed to the main floor and stepped into the foyer. A faint glow from a streetlamp shone through the glass windows that rimmed the door.

He edged forward and looked into the night, seeing nothing that would cause him alarm.

Slowly he backed into the hallway, peered into the living room and dining area and then headed for the kitchen. The refrigerator hummed in the corner. The clock on the wall ticked off the minutes.

Had his mind been playing tricks on him?

He turned the dead bolt on the back door and

stepped outside. His breath hung in the frosty air as he circled the house, checking for anything that might be out of place.

The windows were locked. Shrubbery undisturbed. The wicker rockers and flower pot as he remembered them on the front porch.

Sighing with relief, he returned to the kitchen, satisfied that the sounds had been only the groaning of the old house settling in the night.

Nothing left to do except head back to bed. He passed the door to Sarah's office when the sound of rap music filtered in from the street. Jude stepped into her office and pulled back the curtain.

A gold Eldorado cruised slowly down the avenue.

The car disappeared into the distance.

Jude's eyes flicked over the sidewalk, front yard and property beyond.

Head cocked, ears straining to hear the faintest sound, he waited at the window until the first light of dawn glowed in the night sky.

Only then did he turn from his post, his eyes falling on messages scattered over Sarah's desk.

*Your mom called* was written on each slip of paper.

Jude shook his head. Why wasn't Sarah returning her mother's calls?

He thought of his own dad. Last time they'd

talked was when he'd left home. Maybe he and Sarah shared something in common after all.

The next morning Sarah was ready to do battle with the man sitting at the kitchen table.

She'd tossed and turned most of the night stewing about her selection for the orphanage position. Two weeks ago she would have been thrilled, but everything had changed in the past forty-eight hours. Now she didn't want to leave Atlanta or the kids, and her heart fluttered with agitation every time she thought of pulling up roots and moving on.

How had she gotten into such a pickle? Jude Walker, that's how. He'd knocked at the shelter door and suddenly her world had been thrown upside down.

Frustrated that he'd disrupted her life, she was also tired of his accusations toward Winton Cunningham and was determined to set him straight about a number of things.

Placing the skillet on the burner, Sarah added a heavy dollop of butter and cracked two eggs into the sizzling grease.

"What do you have against Winton Cunningham?" She flashed a peeved glance at Jude, hoping he realized she wasn't sure he deserved a hot breakfast.

"Winton started this shelter," she continued without waiting for Jude to respond. "He bought this building and furnished it with his own money. A year later he turned the operation over to the Caring Heart Foundation. Winton may not fit into your mold, but he's done a lot of good. You could have been a bit more civil to him last night."

Jude visibly bristled. "Are you saying I didn't conduct myself appropriately?"

"Evidently, you haven't read today's paper."

She grabbed a folded section of newsprint off the counter and dropped it on the table in front of him.

"The Metro section ran a piece on Winton and the Caring Heart Foundation that would have encouraged donations, if it hadn't been for three lines in the gossip column."

Sarah pointed her finger at the text in question and read out loud. "The head of the Caring Heart Foundation was seen having a rather heated discussion with a decorated war hero at the Charity Ball last night. Was the situation in the Middle East making them hot under the collar? Or was there something else abuzz?"

"For goodness' sake, Sarah. I don't see how that could harm the shelter. And I stand by what I told you last night. Not only does Winton have a wandering eye, but you've got to admit, his blackmail comment seems suspicious."

Maybe Winton did have an eye for younger women, but that was something he and Elena needed to work out in private. Besides, Sarah didn't want to admit anything to Jude as mixed up as she was feeling right now.

The shelter was in a precarious financial position, and if Jude continued to meddle into Caring Heart business, the limited funding that was available might be withdrawn.

With a huff, she scooped up the eggs, added two slices of toast and plopped the plate in front of Jude. "Your breakfast, Captain."

He turned tired eyes toward her and reached for her hand. "I'm sorry about ruining your evening."

She pulled away. "You're convinced Winton is a womanizer. That upset me."

"I'll give Winton a second chance, okay?" Jude stuck his fork into his eggs and shoved a bite into his mouth. "By the way, great breakfast, Sarge."

She shook her head, suddenly exasperated with herself. No matter what had happened, she needed to cut Jude a little slack. "Church starts in an hour. Are you interested?"

"I'll stay here and take care of the kids," he said.

"The kids will be sitting beside me in the pew. Might be a good opportunity to offer thanks. I'm sure there were times overseas when the Lord protected you from harm."

A telling expression passed over his face. God *had* protected him.

"You want to talk about it?" she asked.

"A roadside bomb. I happened to get there first."

"And saved the lives of your soldiers, no doubt."

He ignored her comment and jammed another forkful of eggs into his mouth.

Okay, so he didn't want to share any of the details. "You can drive your truck and meet us at church, if you'd like."

Jude shrugged. "I planned to spend the day looking for Nicole's sister."

"Last time you got yourself into trouble."

"I won't flash money around, if that's what you're worried about."

Sarah narrowed her eyes.

He placed his fork and knife on the plate. "Okay, I'm sorry. But I'm getting a little frustrated at this maze of dead ends. It shouldn't be this hard to find someone."

"Unless the person doesn't want to be found." The words escaped Sarah's mouth before she had time to reel them in. Jude's face tightened.

Evidently, she'd struck a nerve. Sometimes the truth was hard to accept.

He slipped from the kitchen stool and headed for the door. "See you later."

Sarah let out a sigh as the door closed behind

him. She prided herself on being levelheaded with an optimistic outlook on life, but ever since Jude had appeared on her doorstep, she'd acted as if she'd eaten glass—all sharp edges and cutting remarks.

Now she had a week to tie up loose ends in Atlanta before she caught a plane to San Antonio, which added to her bad mood.

How could a job that seemed like an answer to prayer just a few days ago, now cause her so much concern?

Plus, she continued to find messages that her mother had called. Much as she didn't want to, before she left Atlanta, Sarah and her mom would have to talk.

What would her mother say about the job in South America? She'd probably mimic Sarah's stepfather with his comments about running away.

Okay, so Sarah *had* left the North Georgia Mountains, but for good reason. She couldn't stand by and watch her mother make another mistake when it came to men.

Besides, Sarah's decision to move to Atlanta had led her to Hope House. For the last six months she'd felt a new sense of purpose and belonging. Of course, in less than a week, all that would end and she'd be starting over again.

Hank's comment circled through her mind. Was she running away? From what? Certainly not a dysfunctional homelife with her mother. She'd already left that behind.

No, this time it seemed more like she was afraid of finding something...

*A man to love and love her in return.*

Where had that thought come from?

She closed her eyes and instantly saw Jude dressed in his formal blue uniform, medals gleaming on his chest.

Her eyes popped open. *Silly woman, one night at the ball and you're thinking about glass slippers and living happily ever after.*

She shook her head, hoping to clear away such foolishness. Jude was one hundred percent committed to Nicole.

Sarah needed to focus on that reality instead of how handsome he'd looked last night.

Reaching for his breakfast dishes, she turned as the door opened and Bull stepped into the kitchen.

"Any idea if Jude needs a ride to church?" he asked.

How was she supposed to know? "You'll have to ask him yourself."

Bull raised his brow. "Something going on you want to talk about?"

Sarah turned her back on Bull's questioning eyes and rinsed off the dishes in the sink. "Jude's probably down in the boys' dorm. If you find him, give him directions. Maybe he'll meet us there."

"I thought you'd be on top of the world this morning after being selected for the orphanage position."

Top of the world? Far from it.

She never should have signed the contract. Now she was locked into a position she'd rather not accept.

"I'm just tired, Bull. It was late by the time we got back last night."

"Sure nothing else is bothering you?" he asked.

"Of course not. Give me a few minutes to finish the dishes. I'll meet you at the van."

God's will. That's what she'd wanted.

So why did her stomach clamp down whenever she thought of leaving Atlanta?

Following Bull's directions, Jude found the church and pulled into a parking space next to the shelter's van.

He stepped inside as the last strains of the opening hymn resounded in the sanctuary. The congregation dropped their songbooks back into the racks.

Sarah and Bull stood near the front, bookends to a row of troubled teens.

Jude slipped into the back pew as the minister moved to the pulpit.

"Bow your heads and pray for God's most abundant blessings," the minister began.

Most abundant blessings? From the looks of the humble congregation gathered to pray, the Lord hadn't blessed them with anything in the superlative range. Hardworking folks, no doubt, just trying to make ends meet.

The minister raised his hands. "Father, God of Heaven and Earth, let Your forgiveness fall down on the faithful who stand before You today. Let their hearts be open to accept Your mercy and love."

Where did Jude stand with the Lord? He'd had faith as a child. A misdirected and misguided faith given to him by his father.

But once he was old enough to turn his back on his dad, he'd turned his back on his dad's beliefs in the Lord, as well.

After seeing Sarah in action, he'd begun to realize there might be some good news in the Gospel, after all.

Once again, his eyes sought her in the crowd. Hair falling across her shoulders, Sarah nodded every so often as if encouraging the minister.

A woman committed to Christ. How did she live in the midst of all this pain and not become adversely affected by what she saw?

The minister continued to pray. "Father God, we lift up those who are hurting and seeking direction for their lives."

Jude needed direction to find Nicole. Would Viki know where to find her sister? How was Winton Cunningham involved?

"We pray for all who are troubled by doubt and confusion. Let your mercy touch the brokenhearted, the unloved, those longing to find the completeness that can only be found in You, Lord."

Brokenhearted? Did he love Nicole? How could he be questioning something that offered so much promise six months ago?

"We ask you to wrap your arms around our brothers and sisters and draw them close to You. Amen."

As the congregation took their seats, a woman raised a flute to her lips. Melancholy strains filled the sanctuary with a soul-wrenching tune.

Jude sucked in a deep breath. What had changed in the last couple of days? He'd gotten to know some of the teens. Good kids with troubled pasts. Not too different from the type of kid he'd been. Everyone wanted to be loved and accepted. If the kids couldn't find affirmation and attention at home, they turned elsewhere. Drugs and prostitution were cries for help.

What had Jude done? He'd filled his world with

a drive to succeed, first as he put himself through college and then as he moved up the ranks in the army.

Thankfully, he'd turned the right direction.

Good thief, bad thief. One saw the reality of his sinfulness and asked forgiveness. The other turned his back on the Lord.

Jude couldn't forgive his father. Not after the loneliness he'd experienced as a child.

Crossing his arms over his chest, Jude pushed the memories aside. He had made a new life for himself. He didn't need or want to look back.

After the concluding prayer, the congregation stood for a final hymn. Jude slipped outside and breathed in the crisp winter air.

The noon sun hung high in the sky as the congregation poured from the church. The kids exited first, blinking at the brightness after the subdued interior lighting. Sarah followed, walking between Keesha and Bull.

"I didn't see you in church." Bull slapped Jude's shoulder in greeting.

"I found a pew in the rear."

"Still planning to look for Viki?" Sarah asked.

"If you point me in the right direction."

She turned to Bull. "Take the kids back to the house. Cold cuts are in the refrigerator. They can make their own sandwiches."

Bull waved his hand in the air as he and Keesha herded the kids into the van. "You two keep out of the way of trouble."

A slight breeze played with Sarah's hair. Jude reached out his hand and tucked a wayward strand behind her ear. "You did something different with your hair."

A pink blush tinged Sarah's cheeks. "A little curl, that's all." She shielded her eyes from the sun as she looked into his eyes. "Are you sure you want to do this?"

"I have to find Nicole."

The smile left Sarah's lips. "Of course you do. Let's get in your truck. I have an idea where we should start looking for Viki."

Sarah watched block after block of desolation roll past the window as she and Jude drove through the city.

What she could do with a million dollars. For starters, she'd bail out the shelter and improve the lives of the poor who relied on its outreach.

Winton Cunningham's money could buy a lot of help, but she'd read in the newspaper article that his wealth was tied up in nonliquid assets. That's why the contributions to the foundation were so necessary for Hope House to continue. If only Winton would—

Time to end that thought. He'd been more than generous.

Now Sarah wanted more? She shook her head, feeling a bitterness latch hold deep inside her.

What was wrong?

Concern for the kids, no doubt. What would happen if the shelter were forced to shut down?

Sarah stole a quick glance at Jude. He sat back in the seat, his long legs stretched toward the pedals. With one arm draped over the steering wheel, he propped the other against the window.

"Looks like folks around here could use a little help," he said as they passed a block of homes badly in need of repair.

"It's that cycle of poverty. Breaking free takes effort. A dysfunctional homelife compounds the problem."

"Sounds like you're speaking from personal experience?"

Sarah shrugged. "Money wasn't the issue. My mother was."

"So that's the reason you're not answering her calls."

Maybe it was the fact that she'd just come from church, but Sarah needed to talk.

"My mother kept looking for love, but always with the wrong guy. Guess my homelife wasn't much different from the kids I pull off the street."

"And your dad?"

"He died when I was young."

"I'm sorry, Sarah."

"The tough part growing up was that I never thought my mother wanted me."

"So now you've become the mother you never had?"

"You mean to the teens at the shelter?" Sarah toyed with the sleeve of her jacket. "I don't know if it's the mothering angle or that I can relate."

"You're doing a good job."

Sarah hadn't expected the compliment.

"Since you deal so well with teens, why do you want to move on?" he asked.

Sarah looked out the window at the graffiti decorating the side of a stucco building. "The position was only for six months while Cynthia recuperated from surgery. She's due back at the end of this month. That leaves me without a job."

"Okay, so that explains why you applied for the orphanage position. But what about your dreams for the future?"

"Meaning?"

"A husband. Children."

She didn't like the direction of the conversation.

"Maybe it's not important what I want but what the Lord wants for me."

Jude shook his head. "You know I'm not tuned

in real tight with the Lord, but it would seem to me that God asks us all the same thing. To love one another."

Sarah turned for half a second to stare at the man beside her. He claimed a faltering relationship with the Lord, yet he knew what was important. Love was the key.

Sounded so simple.

Of course, Jude had someone to love.

And Sarah?

She vowed long ago to never repeat the mistakes her mother had made. Plus, she'd didn't want or need anyone in her life.

Then she looked at Jude. Who was she trying to fool?

# EIGHT

Jude followed Sarah's directions and pulled his truck to a stop in front of the motor lodge. Circa 1950, the flashing neon over the office advertised air-conditioning and free TV. A small sign in the window read, Rent By The Hour.

The gutters sagged along the roofline. Paint peeled from the trim, exposing raw wood that buckled in the damp winter air.

"Looks like it should be condemned, Sarah. You sure this is the place?"

She let out a deep breath. "I guess ambience isn't an issue when you're high on meth."

She reached for the door handle.

Jude caught her arm. "Stay in the car while I talk to the manager."

"I'll be okay, Jude," she insisted.

"Would you please do what I say?"

Sarah sighed, but he was glad to see that she settled back in the seat.

"Lock the doors. I'll be out in a minute." Jude left the engine on and the heater running.

The office door needed a paint job as much as the rest of the building. Jude pushed through the entrance.

A slender man with red hair and a patch of goatee looked up from a recliner positioned in front of a portable TV, his hand cocked on the remote. "How many hours you need? I've got two vacant rooms."

"Don't need a room. I'm looking for Viki Valentine."

"Who said you'd find her here?"

Jude paused, remembering the name he'd heard yesterday. "Rashad Sway."

The guy stared at Jude for a long moment. "Last door on the left. Knock three times."

Jude stepped outside. He caught Sarah's eyes, pointed to the end of a row of doors and shook his head as she, once again, reached for the door handle.

No need for Sarah to be exposed to the filth of this dump.

Jude stopped at the last door and rapped sharply. Thick privacy curtains covered the window. Before he could raise his hand to knock again, the door slowly inched open.

"Who you lookin' for?" a raspy voice asked.

Black eyes stared out at him, the pupils dilated. A rash covered the woman's drawn cheeks and scratch marks streaked down her neck. Probably where she'd dug her fingernails into her flesh, chasing imaginary meth mites that crawled beneath her skin.

"Viki Valentine?"

A seductive smirk exposed rotting teeth, the by-product of her addiction. "What do you want, big boy?"

"Information about Nicole."

The smile slipped from her lips. She tried to close the door.

Jude jammed his foot into the opening. "I'm a friend of your sister's. She's disappeared. You've got to help me find her."

The woman cursed, then turned away from the door and slithered into the dark interior of the dingy room. The bed lay rumpled, sheets soiled, the covers thrown upon the floor. Two pillows sagged against the plastic headboard.

He stepped inside, the smell of stale cigarette smoke clouding the air.

"We missed you at the shelter, Viki."

Jude turned to see Sarah standing in the doorway.

"Do you remember me?" Her voice was low and warm as she crossed the threshold.

"Yeah, I remember. You run that shelter on Rosemont Street."

"That's right. We've got space for you at Hope House. Why don't you come back with us?"

The woman shook her head. "I can't leave. If Rashad'd find me, he'd beat me. Maybe worse."

"We won't let Rashad find you."

"I said no." Viki made a shooing gesture with her hand. "Both of you, get outta here. I got business coming."

"Another man, is that it?" Sarah stepped closer.

Viki raised her brow. "Don't you go lookin' down your nose at me with your holier-than-thou attitude."

"We'll give you food and a place to sleep, Viki. You'll be safe."

"Shut up." She covered her ears with her hands, a wild gleam in her eyes. "Leave me be."

"Where's Nicole?" Jude insisted.

Defiantly, Viki dropped her hands and cocked her hip. Raising her index finger, she sauntered toward Jude and jabbed his chest. "You talk to Rashad. He knows all about Nicole."

Jude's gut tightened. "What do you mean?"

"Nicole's one of his girls. She's working for Rashad, just like me." Viki's eyes grew wide, her pupils even more dilated. "Only Rashad set Nicole up in one of those fancy apartments in the Highlands, like she was a princess or something."

Jude shook his head, wanting to cover his ears as Viki had done moments ago.

"You find that sister of mine, you tell her I'm glad I didn't go away with her when she asked me. Who does she think she is? Trying to save me from myself, she says. Wants me to get into rehab. Oh, yeah, Nicole won't do drugs. She's too good for that. Only she's not too good to sell her body to any man who has money to pay her high price."

Anger churned through Jude. "You're making this up."

Viki laughed. "The truth hurts, doesn't it, big boy?"

Jude turned his back on her and headed for the door. Sarah reached out to grab his arm, but he ignored her gesture.

He needed to get away. Away from Viki and her spaced-out attitude, away from Sarah with her penchant for trying to solve everyone else's problems and away from this sleazebag motel where women sold their bodies and their souls.

What Viki said had to be wrong.

"Jude?"

Sarah ran after him. "Viki doesn't know what she's saying. She's angry at her sister, striking out at anyone who reminds her of the mess she's made of her life."

Jude refused to look into Sarah's eyes. He didn't want to see the pity he knew he'd find there. Taking the keys from her hand, he opened the passenger door.

"Get in. I'll take you back to the shelter."

Rounding the car, Jude opened the driver's side and slipped behind the wheel.

Could everything he had believed for the past six months be a lie?

A call girl? He needed to find Nicole to learn the truth.

Sarah rested her head against the back of the seat. What could she say to Jude? Jaw clenched, his hands gripped the steering wheel white knuckled while his eyes scanned the road ahead.

Did he even realize she was in the car?

"Jude, you can't believe anything Viki said."

He threw her a quick glance. "You think she's lying?"

"Meth does terrible things to a person's mind. Viki might not be able to separate fact from fiction at this point."

He laughed ruefully. "She sounded convincing to me."

"Did Nicole act suspicious when you were

together? Or did anything happen that would prove Viki wrong?"

"R&R goes by fast. You know how it is when you're starting to fall in love…."

He turned to gaze into her eyes. Her stomach churned and sadness swept over her.

Sarah had seen what misplaced love could do to a woman. Because of her mother, she had been careful to protect her own heart.

Jude sighed. "I guess I'm saying that when you're in love you don't see things clearly. Reality gets skewed. Know what I mean?"

No, she didn't know. Better to ignore the question than confess the reality of her life.

"You didn't have much time together." Why was she offering excuses?

"Two weeks. I'm beginning to think I didn't know her at all."

Sarah glanced down at the console where Jude had left the commemorative coin found in Nicole's apartment. Sarah touched the shiny enamel. "Yesterday, you mentioned a money clip."

He rubbed his right hand over his jaw, but kept his gaze on the road ahead. "My mother died when I was young. The clip belonged to her dad. I asked Nicole to keep it for me while I was gone."

"It must have been very special to you."

He glanced at Sarah, his eyes guarded. "You

know kids, certain things are important. My mom used to tuck me in bed and tell me she loved me."

Something Sarah never remembered her mother doing.

"We had this little routine going," he continued. "I'd ask her if she was sure, and she'd always reply, 'Cross my heart.'"

"So the money clip was in the shape of a heart?"

He nodded. "With a cross on one side. My mom and her dad started the ritual when she was little. He had the clip made on her first birthday, carried it his whole life and wanted her to keep it after he died as a reminder of his love."

A loving family was all Sarah had ever wanted. She turned to gaze out the window, feeling confusion overwhelm her again. The only love she had ever been sure of was the Lord's.

After all that had happened, she was having trouble accepting even that.

Jude kept his eyes on the road as he drove Sarah back to the shelter. He'd shared too much about his childhood. A moment of weakness, no doubt.

Weakness due in part to what Viki had said. Surely, she had made up stories about Nicole to ease her own twisted conscience. As Sarah had mentioned, drugs did terrible things to people's minds.

Viki *had* to be lying.

Sarah stared out the passenger window, probably thinking about her move to Colombia. For the life of him, he didn't know why she wanted to go to a foreign country when she was doing so much good here in the States.

He doubted she realized the positive impact she had on people's lives. Well, Jude could tell her a few things. One afternoon delivering food to the poor, and he knew she was reaching out to so many people who needed a helping hand.

He saw it in their eyes when they opened the door. Desolate, alone, afraid. But when Sarah smiled, their outlook changed, as if they'd been given a second chance. Sarah brought hope for the future and the will to move forward beyond their present situation.

He'd like to tell her a few things about the way she responded to people's needs, but he doubted she would listen to anything he had to say.

Ever since last night, his relationship with Sarah had become as messed up as his ability to find Nicole.

Two women, both so different, yet both had grabbed a bit of his heart. He'd thought about Nicole for the past six months. Now he could hardly remember what she looked like unless he stared at her picture.

Unconsciously he patted his breast pocket where he kept Nicole's photo.

Sarah turned to stare at him.

When he glanced her way, his breath caught. Forty-eight hours since meeting Sarah, and he wasn't sure of anything. He forced his eyes back to the road, struggling with his mixed-up emotions.

"There's Cynthia." Sarah pointed to a plump African-American woman standing close to Bull as they pulled up in front of Hope House. "She wasn't due back until the end of the month."

Sarah was out of the car and racing up the sidewalk before Jude could pull the keys from the ignition.

"My, my, but aren't you a sight for sore eyes." The older woman wrapped Sarah in her arms.

"Cynthia, this is Captain Jude Walker. He's been helping out for the past couple of days," Sarah said as Jude approached.

The director's face wrinkled into a wide grin. "Bull told me you've been a great help to everyone."

"Nice to meet you, ma'am."

Bull slapped Jude's shoulder and pointed to the sedan parked in the driveway. "If you've got a minute, I could use help with Cynthia's luggage."

"I'll take you to your room," Sarah said to Cynthia. "I know Keesha wants to see you when she gets back from her classes."

As the two women walked arm in arm through the front door, Jude turned to Bull.

"Something on your mind, Captain?"

"I need to talk to Rashad Sway."

Bull shook his head. "That man's nothin' but trouble."

"We found Viki. She said Rashad would know where to find Nicole."

"And you believed Viki?"

"I don't have anywhere else to turn."

"I hear ya. Let's get Cynthia unloaded, then we'll pay Mr. Sway a visit."

Jude noticed the way Bull's eyes warmed when he mentioned Cynthia's name. Looked like he was more than a little interested.

What about Rashad? Would he know Nicole's whereabouts? Or would it be another dead end?

# NINE

"That Mr. Walker certainly seems like a mighty fine young man," Cynthia said, unzipping the suitcase Bull had placed on the bed. "Bull told me he just came back from the Middle East. Imagine him helping out at the shelter. You don't find nice men like that very often."

Sarah reached for one of Cynthia's dresses and hung it in the closet. "He's nice, and very much in love with a lady he's having a hard time finding."

Cynthia raised her brow. "Now, what woman in her right mind would play hard-to-get when someone that handsome was interested?"

"Remember Viki Valentine? She stayed here for a few days about six months ago."

"Just before I had my surgery. Yes, I remember."

"Jude met her sister during his R&R in Atlanta. Now he's back and can't find Nicole."

"Nicole Valentine? I never made the connection between Viki and Nicole."

Cynthia paused in her unpacking and tilted her head. "Winton introduced us about eight months ago. I was meeting a girlfriend from my college days. She's done well for herself and insisted we eat at a little out-of-the-way place she likes in Alpharetta. From the expression on Winton's face, he was as surprised seeing me as I was of seeing him."

"You're sure he was with Nicole?"

Cynthia nodded. "Winton said they were working on an outreach project. She was such a well-dressed, attractive woman, I thought she must have come from a moneyed background."

Despite Viki's accusation, Sarah refused to believe Nicole was involved with anything illicit. But she and Winton could have been involved romantically.

"I didn't want to interrupt their lunch, so we didn't talk long," Cynthia continued.

Sarah chewed on her lower lip, wondering if she should mention what the cleaning lady had said. No reason to spread a story that might be completely innocent. Still, Sarah valued Cynthia's opinion and her good sense of right and wrong.

"Do you think something could be going on between those two?" Sarah finally asked.

"You mean romantically?" Cynthia furrowed her

brow. "Oh, my goodness, no. You know Winton and Elena are happily married."

Sarah felt an instant surge of relief. The question of Winton's fidelity had been troubling her more than she realized. And what about the blackmail comment he'd made?

Winton must have felt threatened by Jude's demand for information about Nicole. Winton's comment had probably been a protective reaction to Jude's confrontation.

"Now, tell me about the orphanage position," Cynthia said as she slipped another dress over a hanger and walked toward the closet.

When Sarah failed to respond, Cynthia placed her hand on Sarah's arm. "You don't look happy. What's troubling you?"

"I…I'm not sure." Sarah turned away from the other woman's steady gaze. Every time she thought of leaving Atlanta, her insides twisted into a dozen knots.

"Could be you're having second thoughts about leaving a lot of things behind? You were a blessing to me, Sarah. When I needed to have my hip surgery, God brought you to the shelter. Quick as a minute, you stepped into a job that most people would be afraid to tackle. I'm grateful. More than you'll ever know."

"But now you're back, Cynthia, and it's time for me to move on to the next job the Lord wants me to do."

"Maybe the job He wants for you and the job you think He wants for you are two different things. You love working with the kids here at the shelter."

Sarah nodded. "But I can't back out of the orphanage position. I signed an agreement when I filled out the application."

"Talk to Winton. He'll understand. I'm sure there are a number of people who would be thrilled to have the job."

Sarah let out a deep breath. Could Cynthia be right?

"After I help you unpack, I'll call him. Last night he said he'd be in his office today, making the arrangements. Hopefully, I can talk to him before everything's in place."

A weight seemed to lift from Sarah's shoulders as she reached for another hanger. Surely someone else could take over the orphanage position in Colombia. Winton would understand that her work at Hope House was important. She'd help at the shelter for as long as Cynthia needed her. At least until Jude tracked down his missing girlfriend.

Was Jude part of the reason she wanted to stay in Atlanta?

"Temperatures will fall to an all-time record low overnight as a cold wave heads south," the weatherman reported over the radio as Jude maneuvered his truck through the Sunday-afternoon traffic.

"Don't be fooled by Rashad," Bull warned from the passenger seat. "He looks like a wimp, but he's one bad dude."

"Who's evidently built quite a network for himself, from what Sarah told me."

"You got that right. Drugs and prostitution mainly. But he's into other things, as well."

"What about the police?"

"Cops keep trying to pin something on him, but the guy's slick, like a greasy pig. Continues to slip through their fingers."

"What about Damian?"

"Word is he's building his own territory." Bull shrugged. "Don't know how it'll play out. Right now, Atlanta PD's focused on Rashad. A friend of my brother's says without Rashad this area might have a chance to spring back to life. The way it is now, Rashad's hand pushes down every attempt at improvement."

"Winton Cunningham doesn't have any problems."

Bull cleared his throat. "You think they're hooking up?"

"Winton seems greasy himself." Jude shook his head. "Maybe it's his wandering eye for women that bothers me."

The corners of Bull's mouth twitched. "You mean Sarah?"

"He was very attentive last night at the Charity Ball."

"Who wouldn't be interested? Sarah's one fine lady."

"Of course she is, but he's a married man."

Bull quirked his brow and regarded Jude for a long moment. "Bothers me to hear he was turnin' on the charm. With Sarah's big heart, she wouldn't know a skunk from a coon dog." A smirk played over Bull's full face. "'Course, sounds to me like you might be a little jealous."

Jude squirmed in his seat. "Jealous? No, of course not. It's just that…"

He tried to find words to express his thoughts, but for the life of him, he couldn't articulate the way he felt. Mixed-up. Confused.

For the past six months he'd been totally focused on Nicole. Now he couldn't get thoughts of Sarah out of his head. He kept remembering the warmth in her eyes and the concern in her voice when she talked to people who were down-and-out. The woman had a big heart, and she wasn't afraid to let her feelings show. She was a genuine person, and she deserved more than working for the likes of Winton Cunningham.

"Sarah needs a family with children of her own," he finally blurted out.

"You're right about that, my man. But she's moving to San Antonio in a week and then on to Colombia."

The finality of Bull's words hit Jude like a live round of ammo. A pain settled in his gut, a sense of loss and loneliness. He tried to shove the feeling aside, but the somber mood continued to hold him in its grasp.

He needed to focus on the task at hand, and that involved confronting Rashad Sway to find out information about Nicole. Jude didn't need thoughts of Sarah getting him off track.

Bull pointed at a small Latino sauntering toward a dilapidated warehouse. "That dude's one of Rashad's men. Looks like we're gonna be able to have a chat with the pig."

When Jude pulled to the curb, Bull rolled down his window and whistled. The Latino turned, one hand reaching for the pistol wedged in the waistband of his jeans.

"What's going down, Jaime?"

The punk's hand relaxed and his face broke into a smile. "*Holá*, Bull. How goes it?"

"*Muy bien*. How's your mama?"

Jaime sidled closer to the truck. "She says you

saved her life. Just like you saved mine. We both owe you."

"You tell her to make sure she lets someone know next time she decides to take a walk around the block."

Jaime glanced down and shook his head. "If you hadn't found her, Bull." He looked up. "She wouldn't have lasted in the cold. Don't know why she decided to go outside when she's so wobbly on her feet."

"Good Lord told me I needed to pay Ms. Rodriguez a visit that day. Didn't know I'd find her facedown in a drainage ditch."

"Why don't you stop by the house? Say hello. She'd like to see you again."

"Your mama's a good woman, Jaime, but she worries you'll end up dead like your cousin."

"Hard to walk away, Bull."

"I did it."

Jaime sucked air through his front teeth. "I remember. You were one bad dude. People still talk about what you controlled. They say if your brother hadn't been killed, you'd run this neighborhood instead of Rashad."

"I made the right decision. You can, too. Get your life squared away with God. He'll lead you." Bull pointed a thumb back at Jude. "Right now, I've got someone who wants to see Rashad."

Jaime shook his head. "Rashad don't want visitors."

"This is important." Bull motioned toward the warehouse. "You go inside. Tell him Bull and his friend are coming in. But I don't want to see any guns. Nobody standing in the shadows. You know what I'm saying?"

"Rashad's not in his office." The Latino glanced away, and even Jude could tell he was lying.

"You want me to tell your mama how you're working for a sleaze pig who uses women?"

Jaime sighed. "Okay, I'll tell Rashad. But only 'cause I owe you."

As the Latino shuffled off toward the warehouse, Bull turned to Jude, voice low. "Follow my lead. Keep your hands exposed. Don't make any sudden moves. And when I tell you to do something, do it."

Jude nodded.

"Now give me your hand."

"What?"

"Your hand, bro."

Jude extended his right hand. Bull grabbed it and bowed his head. "Dear Lord, walk with us into this den of iniquity. Help us face the enemy and keep us safely in your care. Amen."

Last time Jude had tried to pray, an IED detonated around him. Hopefully, this prayer would have less explosive results.

* * *

The warehouse smelled musty and damp with a hint of rotten garbage that wafted past Jude as he and Bull stepped into the dim interior.

Jaime stood just inside the threshold and pointed toward a room at the rear where a sign on the door read, Keep Out.

"Rashad's in his office."

Jude flicked his eyes left to right, searching for some sign of trouble. He'd been on enough patrols to know the enemy could be anywhere.

The warehouse appeared empty except for a black Hummer, white Lexus and steel-gray BMW parked near the rear bay door.

"Nice wheels," Jude said out of the side of his mouth.

"Bought with the money earned from the women he controls," Bull whispered back.

Jude thought of Viki spaced out on methamphetamine, selling her body to earn money to buy her drugs and pay for Rashad's fancy cars.

"Who's with Rashad?" Bull asked the Latino.

"Damian Key."

"What's he packin'?"

Jaime looked down at the floor. "You're askin' too much, Bull."

"I saved your life, *amigo*."

The kid sniffed. "A 9mm Glock on his waist and a .38 strapped to his right leg."

"And Rashad?"

"He keeps a .45 in his desk. Other than that he's clean."

Bull raised his brow. "You telling me the truth?"

Jaime nodded. "Rashad never carries. Lets his men do the dirty work. So he can say he's not involved."

"Not involved, my—" Bull wiped a hand over his mouth. "Okay, Jaime, you go on home now."

The Latino rubbed his fingers over his medal and nervously eyed the closed door with the Keep Out sign. "Rashad told me to hang out."

Bull raised his index finger. "Get outta here."

Jaime nodded. "Just remembered I need to get something at home." The warehouse door slammed as Jaime raced from the building.

"So Damian's still working for Rashad?" Jude asked, his voice low as he and Bull approached the office.

"When Rashad realizes Damian's trying to gain control of his turf, it won't be pretty. Cops are taking bets who'll win in the end."

"Maybe they'll kill each other."

"That's one way to get rid of trouble. Now let's pay the man a visit." Bull raised his hand and knocked twice.

"Rashad, it's Bull."

The door inched open. Damian's face appeared in the slit, his chin scraped and swollen. "What do you want?"

"Move. I need to talk to Rashad. Private like." Bull shoved the door open.

"What the—"

"Shut up, Damian," a voice bellowed from the far side of the office.

Damian hissed as Jude followed Bull into the room. "What's he doin' here?"

Jude squared his shoulders. "Is there a problem we need to discuss?"

"Get out of here, Damian," the voice commanded.

The street punk locked his jaw and let out an exasperated breath, but he left the office, closing the door behind him.

Jude flicked a glance at the man standing beside the mahogany desk at the rear of the room.

Late forties and probably twenty pounds overweight, Rashad Sway was dressed in a high-end silk suit, starched white shirt and striped tie, looking more like a middle-aged businessman than the thug Jude expected.

A phony smile spread over his pudgy face as he stepped forward and extended his hand to Bull.

Rashad couldn't have been over five-ten. Hair

cropped short, he sported a gold stud in each ear and a two-inch scar that zigzagged across his left cheek, the only flaw in an otherwise put-together appearance.

"Long time since I've had the pleasure of your company, Mr. Lejeune."

Returning the handshake, Bull pointed to Jude. "My friend, Captain Walker, just back from the Middle East."

"A pleasure to meet you, Captain."

Jude nodded. "Mr. Sway."

"You'll have to excuse Damian. He has forgiveness issues." Rashad smirked at Jude. "From what I hear, you know how to defend yourself."

"Only when I'm forced."

Lips pursed, Rashad raised his brow. "And the reason for this unexpected visit?"

"I need information about Nicole Valentine."

The hustler propped his hip on the corner of his desk. "Unfortunately, I don't know anyone by that name."

Jude leaned in close. "Don't lie to me, Mr. Sway. You're working her sister out of a motor lodge south of 285."

"Somebody's been giving you bad information, Captain."

Jude thought about what the cleaning lady in

Nicole's apartment had told him. Prime Rental managed the complex, but who owned the property?

"The information I uncovered is that you own the apartment Nicole lived in," Jude threw out, hoping Rashad would take the bait.

A surprised look washed over the hustler's face.

So Jude had stumbled onto the truth.

"What'd you do, spend a little time with Nicole and decide you like the high-price girls?" Rashad asked.

Jude fisted his hands. "She's way out of your league."

"My advice," Rashad pointed his finger at Jude. "You forget about Nicole Valentine and go back to wherever you came from. Wouldn't want a soldier boy who's served his country to get hurt."

"Nicole moved out of her apartment over a month ago. Where'd she go?"

"How should I know?" Rashad raised his hands in the air and shrugged. "Girls like Nicole have a mind of their own. Maybe she met a man she liked more than you."

"Someone who visited her on a regular basis?" Jude suggested. "A rich philanthropist named Winton Cunningham?"

Rashad's jaw tightened. He turned to Bull. "Take your soldier boy and run back to the shelter. You

Christian types shouldn't be around this part of the neighborhood."

"Where's Nicole?" Jude pressed.

"I don't have to tell you a thing."

Bull rubbed his hand over his chin. "You know I still have connections that can cause you harm."

Rashad rounded his desk and slipped into his leather chair. "You don't scare me, Bull. You may have ruled this neighborhood at one time, but you've turned soft."

"I don't mean in the 'hood. I'm talkin' about Atlanta PD. Some of my brother's friends might be interested in checking out a certain video."

"Cops don't have anything on me and you know it."

"That right? Suppose they find a video about a certain killing. Happened a few years ago over in Grant Park."

"Never heard of no video." Rashad's bravado faded along with his pretentious airs.

"Video shows a man attacking a woman while she walked through the park," Bull continued.

"Nobody has a tape like that. Besides, that woman was high on cocaine."

Jude thought of Viki and the way her grandmother said she'd been seduced into addiction.

Crossing his arms over his chest, Jude forced a sarcastic chuckle. "The way I see it, if the police haul you in for questioning, that might give someone else the opportunity to step into your shoes, Mr. Sway." Jude flickered a glance over the top of the desk. "'Course, doesn't look like they're too big to fill."

Rashad flew out of his chair. "Why you snot-nosed..."

"Murder one. Life imprisonment. Maybe even death penalty," Jude ticked off the charges. "That is if the police get hold of the tape Bull mentioned."

Rashad looked from Jude to Bull and back at Jude again. "Nicole Valentine disappeared 'bout a month ago. Okay? No one's seen her since. Talk is somebody wanted her out of the picture."

The words hit Jude in the gut. His throat constricted. He tried to breathe, but he couldn't get enough air.

Bull threw Jude a worried glance, then picked up the slack. "Keep talkin', Rashad."

"I heard a body was dumped in Lake Lament. Not that I'm saying there's a connection."

"You better be telling me the truth, little man, or I'll see that video gets to the police."

Rashad held up his hands, palms out. "No need exposing that tape. Just check the lake. You might find what you're looking for."

Jude headed for the door. His chest ached. He needed air. Bull followed close behind.

Damian stood outside the office, like a guard dog waiting to be called back to his master's side.

Somehow Jude managed to walk across the length of the warehouse and through the door that led to the street. Outside, the cold winter air swirled around him.

He pulled in a shaky breath. "Rashad's lying."

"Stay cool, man, till we get out of this neighborhood."

Jude forced himself to keep moving. Numb as a robot, he crawled into the truck and started the ignition.

As they drove past the warehouse, he let out a shaky breath. "Feels like I'm surrounded by darkness, and I can't find my way out. Everything seems hopeless."

Bull nodded. "Hopeless case? I hear ya. Same way I felt when my older brother died. He was a good cop, moving up the line, getting promotions."

Jude recognized the pride in Bull's voice, as well as the pain.

"He tried to talk me into going clean. Only, I wouldn't listen. One day he was gunned down. Tore me apart. When I found out one of my guys did the job, I didn't want to live anymore."

Bull understood about loss and the heartbreak it could bring. "How'd you survive?"

"God intervened. Gave me what I needed to get

off the street and turn my life around. My brother's friends on the force took me under their wings. Said I was their success story."

No wonder Bull seemed to have influence on both sides of the law. "That's your connection to the police. Yet you still pull a lot of weight with the guys on the street."

"Strange, huh?"

"About as strange as Rashad's reaction when you mentioned the video."

"Picture's too blurred to ID anyone, but rumor has it he killed the woman. The way he reacted today makes me think the cops need to reopen the case. If they put the squeeze on Rashad, might end his reign for good."

"Anyone else come to mind who could provide information about Nicole?"

"A guy I used to deal with has access to phone records. Could be interesting to see who Nicole called before she disappeared."

Jude had come to Atlanta to find a woman he'd known for only two weeks. Had everything about her been a lie?

A high-end call girl. A wealthy sugar daddy who visited her often. A street punk who claimed she was dead.

Underline *claimed*. Who would want Nicole out of the way?

Jude glanced at the big guy. "Even if Rashad's worried about that video, I still don't understand why he divulged information about Nicole."

Bull rubbed his hand over his jaw. "Fear makes men do foolish things. Could be he knows he's on the way out."

Jude's stomach tightened as realization roiled over him. "Or maybe he wants to pull someone down with him. Exactly where's that lake located?"

Bull sucked in a breath. "Not far from here, adjacent to a large estate."

Estate?

The hairs on the back of Jude's neck tingled. "Bet I can guess who owns the property."

Bull's eyes were serious as he glanced at Jude. "If you're thinking Winton Cunningham, then you're thinking right."

# TEN

The drive to Winton's office took fifteen minutes. Once the security guard escorted Sarah into the large complex and announced Mr. Cunningham had a visitor over the intercom, Winton opened the door to his private office and beckoned Sarah forward.

"So glad you stopped by today, my dear. As you know, I usually don't work on Sunday, but the details for your trip to South America needed my attention. Come in and sit down so we can talk." He motioned her toward a Queen Anne chair.

Sarah slipped into the offered seat as Winton rounded his desk and settled into his chair.

"Making plans for the orphanage referral service has been a blessing," he said before Sarah had a chance to explain the reason for her visit. Then, lowering his eyes, he worried his fingers. "Truth be told, I haven't been the best of husbands."

Winton's confession wasn't what Sarah had expected, nor was it a subject she wanted to discuss.

As if sensing her unease, he held up a palm. "Of course, this isn't the time to air personal matters. But the orphanage has been the glue Elena and I needed to hold our marriage together."

"I...I don't understand?"

"Elena can't have children. We wanted a houseful, but our will isn't always God's will."

He raised his brows and glanced pointedly at Sarah. "Something I know you feel strongly about, after reading your application."

"That's what I need to talk to you about."

Ignoring her comment, he continued on. "Elena suffers from depression. Making the initial arrangements so Colombian children can find homes in America has given her a new enthusiasm for life. She even calls the orphans her children."

Feeling empathy for Winton's wife, Sarah thought of her own dreams growing up. Dreams of a husband and family. But now? Just as Winton had said, God's will wasn't necessarily hers.

"I hate to pry, sir, but have you ever considered adopting?"

His face brightened. "We've been talking about that very possibility. In fact, once the agency is established, we want to fly to Colombia to meet the children. With our assets, any children we adopt would want for nothing."

Street urchin to membership in one of the richest of Atlanta families. "You said *children?*"

"Perhaps a brother and sister, or even three siblings who would have to be split up otherwise."

Sarah had come here to tell Winton about her desire to stay in Atlanta, but how could she back out of the agreement when so much good would come from taking the position? "I don't know what to say."

"Say you'll be ready to go by the end of the week. I just completed all the arrangements." He tapped the manila envelope lying on his desk. "Your visa will be mailed to San Antonio. The other information you need is enclosed, along with your airline reservation. Changing at this point would cost more time and money."

Sarah took the packet from his outstretched hand. She couldn't back out now.

An exuberant smile covered his face. He slapped his hands together and stood. "I'll tell Elena we're on schedule. Our twentieth wedding anniversary is in six months. That would be a perfect opportunity to visit Colombia and arrange for our new family. I'll work on the legal arrangements for bringing the children to the States. Elena has kept her citizenship in Colombia, which should speed the adoption process along."

"Yes, of course. By then, we should have a number of children ready to be placed in homes."

"And something else, Sarah. You know I've been worried about Hope House and the decreased funding, so I've decided to sell some of the real estate I own and donate a portion of the money to the shelter, which should help to put us into the black."

"That's so generous of you."

He walked to the edge of the desk. "I've also decided to turn over control of the funds to the director. Cynthia will no longer need board approval on expenditures. Of course, they will still remain as an oversight resource, but the director will have pretty much a free rein. That should expedite services and cut down on paperwork."

Exactly what Cynthia had wanted for so long.

"I'll pass on the good news."

"Tell Cynthia to call me once she gets settled. I can walk her through the new procedures."

Sarah stood, genuinely pleased. Streamlining the process would give the director more free time to work with the kids.

"Cynthia will be thrilled, Mr. Cunningham."

Manila envelope in hand, Sarah said goodbye

and hurried from his office. She needed to get back to the shelter and begin making plans for her trip.

Exciting. Or was it?

She stepped outside and felt her enthusiasm collapse. Six days and she'd leave Atlanta.

As she headed for the van, one question kept niggling through her head.

Why was Winton making such a drastic change in procedure?

The next morning Jude stumbled into the kitchen, headed for the coffeepot and filled a cup with the strong brew.

"Morning," Sarah chirped from the pantry where she was evidently taking inventory. Dressed in a skirt and sweater, she looked fresh and energetic, ready to face the day with a smile.

Bah, humbug. All he could focus on was the possibility of Nicole's body at the bottom of a lake.

The thought made him want to punch a hole in the wall. Last night, when everyone else was in bed, he'd slipped out of the house, climbed into his truck and driven until he ran out of road. His mind numb, he couldn't get past what Rashad had said about Nicole.

As the first light of dawn played over the horizon, he'd returned to the shelter and changed into his running clothes. Ten miles later, he came back for a shower and shave.

Now, cup of coffee drained to empty, he looked once again at Sarah with her sunshine face and sweet smile. The woman could change a monsoon into a spring shower with her sunny disposition.

Did she ever have a problem? Doubtful, except maybe with her mother. Even surrounded by the struggles of Atlanta's poor, she kept an exuberance that was hard to ignore.

Although right now, ignoring Little Miss Sunshine was exactly what Jude wanted to do.

"Sleep well?" she asked.

"Not really." Pouring a second cup of coffee, Jude grabbed a sweet roll from the tray on the counter and turned to leave before she posed more difficult questions he'd have to answer.

Bull charged into the kitchen just as Jude neared the door. He pulled up short and held up his hand. "Whoa, there, big guy. What's happening?"

Bull acknowledged Sarah with a nod, then turned to Jude. "Friend of mine I told you about yesterday couldn't access Nicole's landline so I had him check on Winton's service. He e-mailed me this morning with a listing of the calls made from Winton's private cell."

"And?"

"Up until a month ago, over half of the calls were to a local number." Bull recited the digits. "Sound familiar?"

"The number I dialed every time I got near a phone in the Middle East."

Bull nodded. "The number belonged to Nicole Valentine."

Sarah moved to where they stood. "Winton and Nicole were working on a neighborhood project. Of course there would be phone calls."

Bull shook his head. "Sarah, you don't know the whole story."

Her face tightened with frustration. "Winton and Elena may have had problems in the past, but from what he said when I went to see him yesterday—"

"You did what?" The last place Jude would want any woman to be was in Winton's company, let alone Sarah with her let's-make-everything-perfect outlook on life.

"He turned over control of the Caring Heart funds to the shelter, Jude. No strings attached."

Why did Sarah have to be so gullible when it came to Winton Cunningham? For all the street smarts the woman seemed to possess when she was dealing with errant teens, she was a pushover when the Atlanta magnate was involved.

"Sounds more like he paid you off."

Bull stepped between them. "Jude, we don't have time for this. A friend of my brother's says there might be a little action at Lake Lament this morning."

His gut tightened. "They agreed to drag the lake?"

"Let's just say they're taking a little look-see. You understand?"

Yeah, Jude understood. The cops who Bull had called yesterday would meet them at the lake. And what would they find?

Not Nicole.

*Please, God, not Nicole.*

"I'll go with you," Sarah insisted, seeing the raw emotion written on Jude's face.

Bull shook his head. "Stay here and take care of the kids."

"But—"

They were out the door before she could express her objection.

Sarah gripped the edge of the counter. What were the police hoping to find by dragging the lake on Winton Cunningham's property? Had there been a boating accident?

The back of her neck tingled with apprehension.

Or had they found Nicole?

Grabbing her coat, Sarah raced into the hallway and called up the stairs. "Stay with the kids, Keesha. I'll call you later."

Sarah reached for the doorknob and opened the door.

"Mama?"

There on the porch, hand poised to knock, stood her mother. About the same height and weight as Sarah but with bleached-blond hair combed back in a ponytail, she wore skintight jeans, a turtleneck and matching down vest.

"What are you doing here?"

"We need to talk. I've left messages on your answering machine and cell, but you never returned my calls."

Sarah pushed through the door, forcing her mother to step aside. "This isn't a good time."

She grabbed Sarah's arm. "No time will ever be right, will it? We've got a lifetime of problems to solve. But if you're willin' to listen—"

"Did Hank toss you aside, like the others?" Sarah's voice was bitter.

"Hank wants to start over."

She almost laughed. "What's that mean?"

"We're going to counseling."

Sarah took a step back. For so long, she had prayed her mother would seek professional help. She hadn't expected Hank to be the catalyst.

"He loves me, sugar."

"The question is do you love him?"

"Love isn't always wild and wonderful. Sometimes it's settling for—"

"Health insurance and a pension. That's what attracted you to him in the first place."

Sarah stared at the woman she had tried to please her whole life. Before she could clamp her lips shut, the words that were slamming through her mind shot from her mouth.

"Fact is, Mama, you've never loved anyone."

"Oh, Sarah, I love you more than you'll ever know."

Sarah laughed ruefully. "You never loved my father. You said he was wild and reckless." She saw the question in her mother's eyes. "I overheard you talking on the phone years ago. Only, you didn't know I was listening. Even he wasn't good enough for you."

"Your daddy *was* wild and reckless, but that's why I loved him. When we found out we were going to have a baby, he cried from pure joy. I've never seen a man dote over a child more than he did over you."

Tears stung Sarah's eyes. She swiped her hand across her face, not wanting a moment of weakness to tear down her defenses.

"Why'd you always try to fill the hole in my heart with another man who never measured up?"

"Oh, Sarah…"

Her mother looked away for a moment, as if gathering her courage.

"There was a storm the night your daddy died. Back then, we lived high in the mountains. The roads were slick and treacherous. You'd been sick, and after dinner your temperature went up to 105 degrees. The hospital was over sixty miles away. I called the emergency room. Flu was going around, and the nurse said they were backed up for hours. She told me to give you Tylenol and put you in a lukewarm bath."

Sarah had been so young. She hadn't remembered anything about that night.

"Your dad got in the old pickup we had and raced down the mountain to get the medicine for you. When I heard a car out front, I thought he'd be the one at the door." The words caught in her throat.

"It was the police, telling me he hadn't made the turn at the horseshoe bend. He was alive when they got to him, and he kept repeating your name over and over again."

Tears ran down her mother's cheeks. "It was my fault he died. I'd forgotten to buy the medicine when I'd gone to town earlier in the day. That's why he had to go out in the storm."

Sarah's heart broke with the reality of what her mother was saying.

"The men I ran after…" Her voice was choked with sobs. "They were my way of trying to make it up to you. Over and over again, I asked God why I hadn't been the one in the storm that night. The one who went over the cliff."

All Sarah could do was stare at her mother, broken with the memory of everything that had happened and of the guilt she had carried all those years. The guilt that had kept her from reaching out to her daughter.

Without thinking Sarah stepped forward, opened her arms and wrapped the sobbing woman tight in her embrace.

"It's okay, Mama."

Together they stood on the porch, two women who had been separated, each by a memory too painful to reveal.

At long last Sarah gave in to the tears. She cried for her father who had died that night so long ago, calling out to the child he loved dearly. For her mother who didn't know how to make a life for her child so she turned to men, hoping to find the answers they both needed. Only, she could never find the love she'd lost. So her own sense of inadequacy, her own sense of guilt had created a chasm between mother and child that had nearly destroyed their relationship.

"Shhh," Sarah soothed, rubbing her hand over her mother's shoulder. "We'll make this work."

Then Sarah said the words she had needed to say for a very long time. "I love you, Mama."

* * *

Jude stood on a grassy knoll overlooking Lake Lament and watched as the police boats methodically worked their way back and forth across the water. Their grappling hooks skimmed the murky bottom, occasionally catching on a tree stump or rotten piece of debris.

Morning frost covered the grass, and a westerly wind picked at Jude's Windbreaker. Bull stood a few feet away, his muscular arms crossed over his chest.

Dark clouds rolled across the sky and thunder rumbled in the distance, a warning of the encroaching storm. Two officers standing on the nearby dock stuck their heads in the air and eyed the darkening sky. One of the men glanced at his watch, then scurried up the hill to where Jude and Bull stood.

"Ten more minutes, Bull, and I'll have to halt the operation." He raised his hands and pointed to the dark sky. "Storm's moving in. From the sound of that thunder, it'll hit soon. Don't want my men sitting ducks out on that lake."

"I hear ya, Sam. Appreciate all your help."

Sam double-timed back to the dock.

One of the police boats chugged toward the dock. Sam and his buddy leaned over the water, watching as the men raised the hook.

A bolt of lightning slashed across the sky.

Sam glanced over his shoulder at Jude and nodded.

A body lifted from the water. Strands of long black hair had tangled around the bloated corpse.

Jude's lungs tightened.

The air was heavy with humidity as the storm neared. Overhead, the tall pines bent in the wind, moaning like a keening woman.

Bull placed his hand on Jude's shoulder. "Maybe we should head back to your truck. Let the police deal with this. They'll come talk to us soon enough."

Jude shook off the suggestion.

A second zigzag of lightning cut through the black clouds, but the police ignored the threat, their attention focused on the decomposing body now lying on the wooden dock.

Sam trudged through the frost-crusted grass to where Jude and Bull waited. "The body was weighted down. Doubt we would have discovered her if you hadn't tipped us off. There's something we need to have identified."

Bull's fingers tightened on Jude's shoulder. "Can you do it?"

Jude nodded. Like a dead man walking, he moved forward, his eyes glued on the dock.

Nicole?

Without thinking, he patted his shirt pocket

where he usually kept her picture. For some reason, today he'd left the photo back at the shelter.

But he didn't need a two-by-three glossy to know the Nicole he remembered was warm and vibrant, not the lifeless form stretched over the rough-hewn planks of wood.

Nearing the dock, he flicked a glance at the Cunningham mansion visible in the distance. "Don't try to find me." The words of Nicole's last e-mail circled through his mind. At that moment the clouds opened and rain fell from the sky.

The body couldn't be Nicole's. Surely it was someone else. Nicole's life never would have ended at the bottom of a lake.

An officer approached. "We found this attached to her belt." He held up a plastic evidence bag.

Although the gold heart was partially covered with algae and mud, Jude recognized the money clip he'd given Nicole for safekeeping.

A lump clogged his throat big as a grenade and ready to detonate. Unable to speak, he nodded to the officer, before he pushed forward.

"She's pretty decomposed, sir. Maybe you shouldn't—"

Jude closed his ears to the warning. Fat drops of frigid rain pounded against his face. Jude ignored the odor, ignored the murmurs of the men who stood aside as he walked purposefully to the end of the dock.

An eerie silence settled over the scene, and even the rain stilled for an instant.

Jude stared down at the remains, seeing the oval locket she always wore. Something snapped inside him.

*Oh, God, no!*

The grenade in his throat exploded. He gasped as the gut-wrenching pain cut him in two.

He couldn't breathe, the weight of despair heavy on his chest.

"Her…her name's Nicole," he managed to stammer, forcing the words from his cotton-dry mouth. "Nicole Valentine."

Turning, he shoved through the crowd of cops, needing to get away.

"Wait, Jude," Bull called after him.

A car door slammed.

Jude glanced up to see Sarah standing on the pavement. Even at this distance, he saw pity in her eyes.

Climbing into his truck, Jude jammed the key in the ignition and stepped on the gas.

The last thing he heard was Sarah calling his name.

# ELEVEN

Sarah pulled her eyes from the news update on the television and glanced at the clock on the kitchen wall. Where was Jude?

She and Bull had driven back to the shelter two hours ago. Why hadn't Jude called to say he was okay?

At least her mother had arrived home safely. Home to Hank. If the counseling worked, there might be a happy ending on that front after all.

A surge of hope warmed Sarah's heart when she thought of her renewed relationship with her mother. A heavy weight had lifted from her shoulders in that regard, but it didn't ease her concern for Jude.

As she eyed the clock once again, the back door blew open and Jude stepped inside. Blood crusted his cheek, and an ugly gash snagged the corner of his mouth.

She drew in a sharp breath. "What happened?"

His eyes focused on the portable television, sitting on the counter.

The newscaster's voice filled the kitchen. "The body pulled from Lake Lament appears to have been submerged for four to five weeks. We'll be back with another update later in the broadcast."

Sarah moved to Jude's side as the station went to a commercial break. "I'm so sorry about Nicole."

He stared at Sarah for a long moment, his eyes guarded, brow furrowed. Then he wiped his hand over his chin. His knuckles were scraped and bruised.

The rain had ended earlier, but the temperature had dropped, and a swirl of damp, frigid air blew in through the door that hung open behind him. Sarah reached around Jude and shoved it closed.

"There's a fresh pot of coffee. I'll get you a cup while you wash up."

"You don't have to help me, Sarah." His voice rang with anguish.

"Use the sink in here. The kids will be home from school soon. I don't want them to see you like this."

Reaching for the faucet, she adjusted the water temperature. "Winton's name's been all over the news. He hasn't been charged yet, but the police are holding him for questioning."

"He's involved, Sarah."

Winton and Nicole may have been having an affair, but Sarah couldn't believe someone who had done as much good as Winton could be capable of murder. This wasn't the right time to express her feelings to Jude. He'd been through so much already.

"Is that your blood or the other guy's?" she asked, eyeing the blotch on Jude's cheek.

Then she shook her head and pulled a ceramic mug from the overhead cabinet. "Forget it. I really don't want to know."

"I didn't start the fight."

"From the looks of your lip and those knuckles, you must have taken on everyone you could find."

"I went looking for Rashad, but I found Damian."

When he finished at the sink, Sarah handed him the cup of coffee and a tube of antibiotic ointment from the first-aid kit. "Ever consider turning the other cheek?"

"You weren't there, Sarah."

"Meaning what?"

"Meaning you don't know how it played out. Damian wasn't alone."

She put her hands on her hips. "How many guys did you go up against?"

He smeared the ointment over his knuckles. "That's not important. The important thing is what

I learned. Looks like Rashad wanted Nicole to end the affair with Winton and killed her when she refused."

"Is that fact or merely Damian's take on the situation?"

Jude shrugged. "It sounds plausible."

"But wouldn't hold up in a court of law." Sarah turned away, frustrated that Jude would believe anything Damian said.

Jude placed a hand on her shoulder. "I know it's hard to accept that Winton might be involved."

Before she could respond, Bull charged into the kitchen, holding the phone in his right hand. He pointed to the cut on Jude's lip with his left. "How's the other guy?"

"Make that plural. Damian's friends are wishing they never got involved."

"I hear ya." Bull handed the cordless to Sarah. "It's Viki Valentine's grandmother. She sounds upset."

"I'm so worried," Opal cried when Sarah raised the phone to her ear. "Viki saw the news and claims Nicole's death is her fault. She's run through her money and her drugs, but she found a bottle of aspirin and says she wants to kill herself. You've got to find her."

Sarah quickly reassured Opal before she hung up and repeated the information to Jude and Bull.

"Let's check out that motor lodge we visited yesterday. I'll drive," Jude said. "Take your first-aid kit. We might need it. Bull, call the EMTs and tell them to send an ambulance."

Jude stretched out his hand to Sarah, giving her an encouraging nod when she hesitated.

She grabbed her coat and first-aid kit, then slipped her hand into his, feeling the strength of his grip.

"Keesha's in class and Cynthia's at a doctor's appointment," Sarah said to Bull as she and Jude stepped toward the door. "Get the kids settled, then follow us to the motel."

A news report flashed over the television screen. They turned to catch the update.

"A late-breaking report," the announcer said. "Fulton County police have confirmed that the woman pulled from Lake Lament was Nicole Valentine. A preliminary medical exam verified she was three months pregnant."

Jude maneuvered the pickup south on Moreland and tried to focus on the traffic, but the news announcer's words kept pounding through his mind.

Nicole pregnant?

The reality hit him like a double punch and threatened to suck the air from his lungs.

He'd been so wrong about their relationship. To

him R&R had been the start of something wonderful. Yet their time together had meant nothing to Nicole.

He flicked a glance at Sarah. She'd talked about her mother's string of men. He could relate. No denying the truth any longer. He'd been one of *many* men in Nicole's life.

Heavyhearted, he watched the minutes tick off the clock on the dashboard. He needed to push aside the mixed-up feeling that churned through his gut and concentrate on the problem at hand—getting to Viki in time.

He thought of the innocent little boy he'd held in his arms. Jude knew all too well what it was like to go through life without a mom. Shawn needed his mother.

Viki had made a ton of mistakes, but so many circumstances played into the mix. Getting hooked on drugs was at the top of the list.

What about Nicole? Had circumstances propelled her into a lifestyle she otherwise never would have chosen?

Three days ago Jude had come to Atlanta thinking he'd find the woman he thought he loved. Instead he'd uncovered an ugly web so tangled that he had no idea where it would end.

"There's the motel," Sarah said, when the motor lodge appeared in the distance.

Jude listened for sirens, but he heard nothing except the sound of barking dogs and the downshift of a delivery truck that passed just before he turned into the near-empty parking lot. He braked to a stop outside Viki's room, grabbed the first-aid kit from the console and raced to the door, Sarah close behind.

Pounding his open palm against the peeling paint, he shouted, "Open up, Viki. It's Jude Walker and Sarah Montgomery."

When no one answered, he nudged Sarah out of the way. "Stand back."

Just as he was ready to throw himself against the door, it swung open.

The clerk with the red goatee motioned them inside. "She says she took a whole bottle of pills."

Jude rushed to where Viki was doubled over on the floor. He touched her shoulder and pulled her head back to stare into her glazed eyes.

Sarah reached for the empty bottle on the nightstand. "Full-strength aspirin, 325 milligram. Three hundred count."

Enough to kill two people.

"We need to induce vomiting. There should be some ipecac in the first-aid kit," Jude said.

Finding the vial, Sarah pulled off the lid. "The instructions say to follow the dose with warm water." Sarah grabbed a glass and ran to the sink.

Jude held the bottle to Viki's lips. "Swallow this. It'll make you sick, but you've got to expel the pills you took."

She gulped the ipecac followed by the water Sarah offered.

"Help me get her into the bathroom." Jude glanced around, looking for the motel clerk.

"He left." Sarah gripped Viki's left elbow. Jude wrapped the woman's right arm around his shoulder and lifted her to her feet.

Together they walked toward the latrine, dragging Viki between them. Her step was unsure, her eyes heavy.

"Come on, you can do it," Sarah encouraged.

Head drooped to her chest, Viki moaned in response.

Where was the ambulance?

Jude guided her toward the toilet and held her head as the ipecac began to work. The shrill wail of a siren sounded in the distance.

"How's she doing?" Bull stormed into the motel room just ahead of the EMTs.

"Surviving, at the moment." Jude quickly explained what he'd done when the medical personnel arrived.

"Is someone willing to follow us to the hospital and get her checked in?" an EMT asked once they had Viki stabilized and on the stretcher.

"I will," Sarah quickly volunteered.

Jude looked at Bull. "I need your help, buddy, to find Rashad."

"Count me in."

Jude watched the emotions play over Sarah's face as the EMTs rolled Viki toward the ambulance. Sarah was such a good person who cared deeply for others.

Jude had been a fool. Six months ago, he'd fallen in love with the wrong woman.

Viki was initially treated in the E.R. and then moved to a room on the second floor. Now, standing at her bedside, Sarah waited silently as the doctor reviewed her chart and once again checked her vital signs.

An IV hung next to Viki's bed, sending life-giving fluids into her vein. The steady beep of the heart monitor recorded her pulse, blood oxygen level and heart rhythm. Although she wasn't out of danger, her prognosis was good.

The doctor made a note on her chart before he looked down at his patient over the top of his reading glasses.

"Good Lord was watching out for you today, Ms. Valentine. You had a close brush with death. We'll keep you for seventy-two hours. After that, it's your decision. You can walk out of here on your own and go back to what your life has been. Or you can agree to rehab. We'll see what we can do to get you into a good program."

Although still lethargic, Viki seemed to understand the importance of what the doctor was saying.

"You think I can get the monkey off my back?" she asked, her voice weak.

"Depends on you. If you're serious and committed…" The doctor looked into her eyes. "I won't sugarcoat the reality of rehab. It's a long, hard road." He glanced at Sarah. "But if you've got people to support you."

Sarah nodded encouragingly to Viki and squeezed her hand. "You've got your grandmother and Shawn to think of, as well."

A tear ran down Viki's cheek. "My baby don't deserve a mama like me."

"You're right," the doctor said with honesty. "He needs a mother who's drug free. But that *can* be you, if you give rehab a chance."

She nodded. "I'll do more than give it a chance. I promise you, I'll make it work."

That's what Sarah had been waiting to hear. "Everyone at Hope House will help, Viki. You won't be alone."

"Sounds like you've got the support you need." The doctor smiled. "I'll check on you a little later,

Ms. Valentine. Best thing right now is for you to get some rest."

When he left the room, Viki turned tired, worried eyes to stare at Sarah. "You've got to pray for me. Tell the Lord I'm sorry for what I did."

Sarah patted her hand. "I will pray for you, Viki, but you can tell Him yourself. You may have turned your back on the Lord, but He hasn't turned his back on you."

Viki tried to smile, but it seemed as if the effort demanded more energy than her body could muster.

"Everything would have been okay," she mumbled, her eyes drooping, "if I hadn't stolen the photos of Nicole and Mr. Cunningham."

Sarah gently nudged her shoulder. "Tell me what happened."

Viki wiped a hand over her face, as if trying to clear her mind. "Mr. Cunningham came to the motor lodge. I told the night clerk not to tell anyone where I was. But—"

"Go on," Sarah encouraged.

"Mr. Cunningham said Nicole wanted me in rehab. I was high on meth and didn't want anyone tellin' me what to do."

"What about the photos?"

Before she could answer, Viki's eyes closed and her breathing eased into the methodic rhythm of deep sleep. Sarah tried to nudge her awake but to no avail.

Had Viki found pictures of Nicole and Winton that revealed something about their relationship? Winton mentioned blackmail when he talked to Jude.

As addicted as Viki was to methamphetamine, surely she couldn't have masterminded the scheme.

Who else had been involved? Rashad?

Leaving the hospital, Sarah pulled her cell from her purse and called Bull. When he failed to answer, she left a message, explaining about Viki's condition and the photos she'd mentioned.

"Rashad could have been involved in blackmail so be careful," Sarah warned.

Before she disconnected, another call beeped in. By the time she clicked over, the call had gone to voice mail.

"Sarah, this is Elena Cunningham. I must talk to you about the Caring Heart Foundation. Would you come to my house, please?"

Hearing the anxious tremble to Elena's voice, Sarah's heart went out to the woman who seemed to be an innocent victim in the middle of this terrible situation. The least she could do was make a quick stop at the Cunningham estate before she headed home to Hope House.

Home. Exactly what the shelter had become.

She thought of her move to Colombia. After all that had happened, she no longer trusted Winton or the plans he had for the orphanage referral agency.

With the shelter strapped for financial support, Sarah needed to stay in Atlanta and help however she could.

She didn't want to leave the kids.

She didn't want to leave Jude, either.

# TWELVE

Sarah eased the van along the access road that headed toward the Cunningham mansion and the lake beyond. Overhead the sky had turned an angry black, signaling the approach of a second band of winter storms.

Sarah upped the heat and gripped the steering wheel as the wind tugged at the car. In the distance, the lake looked dark and foreboding. Small waves lapped against the dock where Nicole's body had lain after being pulled from the water.

Sarah's heart broke, thinking of the beautiful woman in Jude's photo and the pain he must have experienced watching her body rise from the murky depths.

At the side of the road, a highway sign shimmied in the wind. Dead End was stenciled in black letters on the fluorescent yellow background.

Exactly how Jude must feel. He'd come to Atlanta expecting to start his new life with Nicole, never imagining it would end before it even had a chance to begin.

Parking the van on the far side of the circular drive, Sarah braced against the wind and pulled her coat up around her neck as she scurried toward the door. She lifted the brass knocker and tapped twice.

Elena opened the door, eyes guarded, hair pulled into a bun at the base of her neck. She tried to smile, but the attempt fell short.

"Come in. It is cold outside. I will make a cup of tea for us."

Sarah wiped her feet on the welcome mat and stepped into the huge foyer, admiring the circular staircase and glittering chandelier that hung over the marble floor. Beyond the entryway, she noticed the expansive great room decorated in ornate French Provincial furniture.

Elena motioned her toward a royal-blue sofa. "Winton told me you found a problem with the financial statement for Hope House," she said once they were both seated. "You did not tell anyone about this?"

Elena seemed as concerned as Sarah was about the shelter. "No, of course not."

"Soon you will leave Atlanta for the language school, yes?"

Sarah shook her head. "I can't go, Elena. I need

to stay here and help at the shelter. Winton mentioned the decline in contributions, and I'm worried Hope House might have to close. Someone else will have to take my place in Colombia."

Elena patted Sarah's hand. "I will call Winton and tell him to come home so you can talk about your change of plans."

"But isn't he at police headquarters?"

Elena studied Sarah for a long moment. "He is now at his office. You will wait here? I will use the phone in the kitchen while I make the tea I promised you."

"I'm sure Winton has other things on his mind right now," Sarah said.

"Do not worry. Everything will be better soon."

When she left the room, Sarah settled back against the plush cushions. The sound of Elena's voice filtered into the living room. She was talking excitedly to someone on the phone. Winton, no doubt.

In a few minutes she returned, carrying a tray with two cups of tea, sugar, cream and wedges of lemon, and placed it on the table in front of the couch.

"This is a special brew. It may seem bitter at first. You must add a little sugar. I hope it will be to your liking."

Sarah took the offered cup. "Is the tea from your country, Elena?"

She smiled. "Yes, of course."

Sarah added two spoonfuls of sugar and a dollop of cream before she sipped the hot beverage. Elena was right, even with the extra sugar, the underlying bitterness was noticeable.

Elena took a long swig from her own cup. "Hot tea is good on a cold day."

Sarah took another sip of the bitter brew. "Winton said your friends and relatives in Colombia have made donations to a special fund for the referral agency."

"That is correct. I am the treasurer for the project and—"

"I didn't know you had a financial background."

"My degree is in accounting. Winton did not tell you that I do the books for the Caring Heart Foundation?"

Why hadn't Winton told her Elena handled the funds?

"But you didn't know about the financial problem I uncovered just a few days ago?" Sarah asked.

"The first Winton mentioned it was at the Charity Ball."

Was Elena telling the truth? How could she not know about the problem?

A ringing filled Sarah's ears. Elena's voice seemed far away. What was she saying?

"I'm sorry, Elena, but I'm feeling very strange."

Sarah lifted the cup and saucer from her lap and placed it on the table. The porcelain teacup wobbled on the saucer, then fell to the floor. She wanted to grab a napkin from the tea tray to mop up the spill, but her arm wouldn't respond.

Her heart raced as she realized what was wrong. "You put something in my tea."

Before Elena could answer, a rap-tap-tap echoed through the house. She stood and walked to the door.

Sarah pushed her hands against the cushions and tried unsuccessfully to rise from the couch.

Who was at the door? Winton?

Surely he would help her.

Elena cracked open the door, and a man slipped inside. He spoke rapidly to Elena, his back to Sarah.

"Help me!" she screamed.

He turned and glared at Sarah.

Her heart did a slow slide against her rib cage.

Rashad Sway.


Jude braked to a stop outside the warehouse and reached for Bull's hand. "Make it fast."

"Father," Bull prayed. "We're asking for justice not vengeance. Let the truth win out."

"Amen."

Jude glanced around as they entered the expansive interior. The BMW and Lexus were parked in the rear. No Hummer in sight.

The door with the Keep Out sign hung open. "Empty," Jude announced once he peered inside the office.

Footsteps sounded over his shoulder. He turned and spied Roy Valentine, sliding a push broom across the cement floor.

He was clean-shaven and had donned what looked like a new pair of khaki slacks, wool sweater and a Windbreaker. Although he slumped forward and his steps were slow, he appeared clear-eyed and alert. Not the drunk Jude had confronted at the overpass.

"What are you doing in Mr. Sway's office?" Roy demanded.

"If you're working for Rashad now, you're working for the man who killed Nicole," Jude said.

"Nicole was Rashad's girl. He wouldn't kill her and lose all that money rolling in from the high-paying johns."

"Unless she wanted to leave him."

Roy's eyes narrowed. "Why would she do that? She had everything a girl could want. Money. A nice place to live. Even vacations at fancy hotels where she could pick up more business." Roy shook his head. "Except she made a big mistake six months ago when she met you."

Roy pointed to Jude. "Whatever happened at Lake Lament, you started it all. You came into Nicole's life. After that, everything went bad for her."

How could Jude have been responsible for what happened to Nicole? "Where's Rashad?" he demanded.

"He raced out of here in his Hummer. Jaime left at the same time. That's all I know."

Jude nodded knowingly to Bull. "We need to find Jaime."

Sarah tried to focus on what Elena and Rashad were saying.

"Get rid of her." Elena made a dismissive motion with her hand. "She knows about the missing funds."

"But you said the problem would be solved when she moved to Colombia."

"How was I to know she would change her mind?"

Had Sarah been selected for the orphanage position because of the financial error she'd uncovered?

"Besides, blackmailing my husband was not part of our agreement."

Rashad pointed his finger at Elena, his voice stern. "The deal was I supply your pills. You don't question anything else."

He turned and glared at Sarah, then walked purposefully toward her. She clawed at the cushions, trying to get away, but he grabbed her arms and yanked her upright. Her legs buckled, and she crumbled to the floor.

Wrapping his arm around her shoulder, once again Rashad forced her to her feet and dragged her toward the kitchen door.

"Make sure you dispose of her car," Elena warned.

Sarah tried to make sense of what was happening, but her mind was as unresponsive as her limbs.

Elena had spiked her tea. Is that what had happened to Nicole?

The lake. Would she be dumped into the frigid water to die in the same way?

She had to keep her eyes open. But at that moment her world went black.

# THIRTEEN

Following Bull's directions, Jude drove the truck along a series of back streets lined with cottages that had long ago fallen into disrepair.

"Jaime lives there." Bull pointed to a small house with a wraparound porch and giant oak in the front yard.

Jude pulled the truck to the curb and rolled down the window as the young Latino came through the front door.

"Where's Rashad?" Jude demanded.

Approaching the truck, Jaime hunched down and peered through the open window. He acknowledged Bull with a nod before he turned his gaze back to Jude.

"Whatever you two said to him yesterday has him scared." Jaime shook his head. "Never seen him like this. He's worried."

"Did Rashad tell you where he was going?"

"Just that he had business. He took the Hummer. Wouldn't let me go with him. Said he needed to handle it himself."

Bull rubbed his chin. "Is there something else you want to tell us, Jaime?"

The Latino shuffled his feet. Finally he leaned closer and lowered his voice. "Rashad's got a place in Little Five Points and a new woman. Not one of his girls, but someone he keeps for himself. People say that's why he's going soft."

"Where's she live?"

"One block west of Moreland. Real pretty place with gas lights on the porch. She keeps 'em burning day and night."

Jude nodded. "Thanks, Jaime. That's a help. Now do what Bull told you yesterday. Get out of Rashad's clutches, and make a new life for yourself."

The Latino's eyes grew wide. "Don't know if I can. Unless somebody takes Rashad off my back."

Jude nodded. "Seems a lot of people feel the same way." He glanced at Bull. "We'll see what we can do, but we need evidence the police can use against Rashad. If you think of anything else, let us know."

Jaime nodded. "Will do."

Jude rolled up his window and turned to Bull. "How do we get to Little Five Points?"

Fifteen minutes later, they entered a bohemian-looking area that could have doubled for a sixties stage set, complete with a cast of flower children, sporting punk hair and body piercings. The modern-day hippies wandered aimlessly along the street, passing shops that hawked an assortment of bongs and other drug paraphernalia. A tattoo parlor sat midblock, its facade painted black with a ghoulish skull and crossbones over the door.

Jude turned onto one of the side streets. One block west of Moreland, the area turned residential, a mix of upscale homes tucked between less privileged properties.

"There." Jude pointed to a two-story Charleston home with a wide porch, wicker furniture and gas lights.

He parked in the driveway and peered into the garage as they passed by. "One sports car. No Hummer."

"Let's introduce ourselves to the girlfriend." Bull headed for the back door. "Maybe she'll know where we can find the pig."

Jude knocked twice and pulled in a sharp breath as the door opened. "Elena?"

The woman smiled. "People say we look alike. I am Odilia. You know my aunt?"

Same regal bearing, wide eyes, oval face, long

black hair. Now that he looked closer, Jude realized this woman was younger. Probably late twenties.

"We're looking for Rashad Sway." Without being obvious, Jude placed his foot across the threshold in case Odilia's hospitable nature changed once her boyfriend's name was mentioned.

"I'm sorry, but he is not here."

From her open expression, Jude doubted Odilia had any idea of what Rashad's life really entailed. The hustler had probably conned her into believing his business was legit.

How long would it take until Rashad pulled Odilia down into the muck and mire that surrounded his life, just as he had done with so many other women, including Nicole?

Jude expected a sharp pain of grief to cut through his heart. Instead he felt only the sadness.

What he and Nicole had shared for two weeks hadn't been based on truthful reality.

Sarah was different. She was real. Not someone locked in lies.

A sense of concern swept over him.

He and Bull said goodbye and hustled back to the truck. Once he started the engine, he turned to Bull. "Call Sarah. See if she's left the hospital yet."

Bull eyed him for half a second before he pulled his cell from his pocket. "There's a voice mail."

Bull listened to the message, then held the phone

out to Jude. When he heard Sarah say she was stopping by the Cunningham estate, an anxious shiver scurried down his spine.

"Call the shelter. See if she's back."

Bull's face tightened when he spoke to Keesha. "No one's seen Sarah."

Jude pulled to a stop in front of the Wintons' mansion. The lake sat behind the house, an ominous reminder of all that had happened.

The wind had teased a shutter loose that banged back and forth against the stucco facade, sounding like a death knell in the encroaching storm.

Jude pounded on the door, then shielded his eyes and peered through the etched windows that edged the doorframe.

No movement. No sound. No indication anyone was inside.

Frantic to find Sarah, he raced around the house and tried the kitchen door, then the sliding glass on the patio. Both were locked.

As he returned to the front, Bull's cell rang.

"Yeah?" The big guy turned from the wind, the phone close to his ear. "You sure, Jaime?" He nodded. "I hear ya."

Bull snapped the phone shut, his brow furrowed with worry. "Something's going down. Jaime was on the phone with Rashad and heard someone in the office mention Sarah's name."

Before Bull could say another word, Jude was in the truck, key in the ignition. Bull scooted into the passenger seat.

Driving without regard to the speed limit, Jude thought only of Sarah's safety. Why had one of Rashad's goons mentioned her name? A number of explanations flashed through his mind, none of them good.

"Turn left at the next corner." Once again Bull reached for his cell. He plugged in a number and lifted the phone to his ear.

"Antwahn, my man. How goes it?" Bull paused for the reply.

"Need you to do me a favor. You know that warehouse Rashad Sway calls his office? See who's hangin' round. Let me know if Damian's keepin' Rashad company. Call me back."

An icy drizzle began to fall. Jude flipped the wipers to low. The droplets thickened and began to stick to the windshield. Jude shoved the heater to high. "Weather report said we're in for snow flurries later tonight."

"Forget about getting anywhere fast if that happens. First sign of snow and Atlanta shuts down," Bull said.

His cell rang again as the warehouse came into sight.

"Yeah, Antwahn. What's happenin'?" Bull listened. "Got it."

He turned to Jude. "Damian just left. Rashad's alone."

"Can you trust Antwahn?"

"I helped him out of a jam a few months ago. He's not real bright, but he tells the truth."

Jude pulled to the rear of the warehouse, cut the engine and looked at Bull, brows raised. "Prayer?"

The big guy nodded, and they both reached for their respective door handles. "Keep us safe, oh, Lord, we pray."

A cold blast of air swirled around Jude. He raced toward the building. Bull followed. Inside, Rashad's three vehicles were parked in a row. Jude edged around the Hummer and peered into the other two cars. Empty.

A phone rang from Rashad's office. Someone answered, grunted a few words, then hung up.

Leading the way, Jude glanced at Bull before he turned the knob and stepped into the office.

Rashad shot out of his chair and jerked open the top drawer on his desk, exposing a .45 automatic. His hand rested on the weapon, his eyes, like black coals, smoldered with rage.

"What the—"

"Where's Sarah?" Jude demanded.

"I don't know who you're talking about."

"You're lying. You know she runs Hope House. One of your thugs mentioned her name while you were on the phone."

"So now I have a snitch working for me? How interesting."

Jude stepped toward the desk. "Where is she?"

A chrome-plated .45 came out of the drawer. "Chill, Captain."

Bull caught Jude's arm and held him back. "Best do as the man says."

With a .45 pointed at his chest, Jude weighed his options. Brute force wouldn't win out in this scenario. He needed to keep talking and throw Rashad off track.

"If you won't tell me about Sarah, what about Nicole Valentine? She worked for you. But something went wrong. She wanted out, didn't she, Rashad?"

"I told you before, I didn't have anything to do with Nicole's death."

Footsteps sounded in the warehouse. Jude shot a glance over his shoulder. Winton Cunningham stood in the door, snub-nose .38 in his right hand.

"What an eclectic gathering." Winton's suit was rumpled, his hair uncombed. "I'm surprised Damian's not here. But then, I heard you two have parted ways."

Rashad pursed his lips, a sour expression on his face.

"Seems there's a little friction brewing," Jude said, adding fuel to the fire. "Damian's trying to set up his own turf."

"And from the talk on the street, evidently he's succeeded," Bull chimed in.

Rashad bristled. "Damian's coming back. You can count on that. Put your piece away, Winton. I don't want anyone hurt."

"You didn't care about hurting Nicole." Winton ignored the order and stepped into the office.

"Why would I kill Nicole? She was one of my best girls. Doing the high-end escort jobs, making good money."

Jude fisted his hands. "Why you—"

Bull grabbed his arm. "Let them talk." His voice was low so only Jude could hear. "We might learn what went down."

Oblivious to Bull's comment, Winton continued. "You killed Nicole because I ran out of cash and could no longer make your blackmail demands, isn't that right, Rashad? Did Nicole tell you she was carrying my child?"

An evil smile broke out on the hustler's puffy

face. "Of course I knew. But I got rid of her body to protect your wife."

Winton stepped closer. "You're scum. How dare you bring Elena into this."

"Ever wonder who supplies those uppers she pops like candy?" Confident now, Rashad cocked his head. "Gotta feed the habit, know what I mean? She said you found out about the money she embezzled."

Realization registered on Winton's face. "Elena used Caring Heart funds to pay for her drugs?"

"Ask her yourself." Rashad pointed to the door.

Meticulously groomed and carrying an oversize leather handbag, Elena stood in the doorway.

"Go home, Elena, we can talk later. I know what he's saying about you is a lie."

"Then you are more of a fool than I thought, Winton."

He glared at his wife. "I demand that you leave this minute."

"How ironic. Since you were leaving me. Rashad showed me the photos of you and Nicole together. That night, I told you I was staying with my niece. But I was still home when Nicole came to meet you. You were looking for her sister so the three of you could go away together."

"Nicole insisted I find Viki."

"You made the mistake of falling in love. And she made the fatal mistake of getting pregnant. The child we always wanted but I could not give you."

Elena's voice was cold as the wind that howled through the warehouse. "Nicole was crying when she talked to me that night. She did not love you, Winton, but she wanted a better life for her baby. I fixed her a cup of tea laced with the pills Rashad gave me. A special potion—"

Jude had heard enough. He caught Bull's eye and whispered out of the side of his mouth. "On the count of three."

Bull nodded almost imperceptibly.

"One."

"Rashad said he would get rid of Nicole's body," Elena admitted. "I did not know he would dump her in the lake."

"Two."

"What better place?" Rashad walked to the front of his desk, a conniving sneer on his face, the gun still pointed at Winton. "I needed to teach you a lesson."

"Three."

Jude crashed into Rashad. Caught by surprise, the hustler staggered backward. Jude fought for control of the .45.

Bull tackled Winton. The snub nose went off in their struggle. The bullet hit Rashad in the shoulder. He fired back. Blood sprayed from Winton's chest as he collapsed onto the floor.

Jude jabbed his fist into Rashad's gut and knocked the .45 across the floor.

"Where's Sarah?" Jude demanded.

Rashad sneered. "I'll never tell you."

"Why you lousy—" Grabbing Rashad's lapel, Jude slammed him against the wall. "Where'd you take her?"

"She's still alive. But hurt me, and she'll be gone for good."

Rashad glanced over Jude's shoulder. Fear flashed in his eyes. "No, Elena."

Jude turned and saw the revolver she pulled from her purse.

"Move away, Captain Walker. I do not want to injure you."

Bull rose to his feet. "Elena, you listen to Bull. You don't want Rashad's blood on your hands."

She shook her head and waved the gun at Rashad. "He knew Winton and Nicole were having an affair, yet he did nothing to stop them."

Jude lunged for the gun, but she squeezed the trigger.

The bullet exploded past Jude and hit its mark.

Rashad jerked as a gaping hole ripped open his side. He slithered down the wall.

Bull rushed Elena and grabbed the revolver from her hand.

Jude knelt over Rashad. "Tell me where you've got Sarah?"

"You'll never…find…her," he gasped as the life ebbed from him.

"No!" Jude screamed. He looked from Elena, now sobbing in Bull's arms, to Rashad's dead body.

He kept seeing Sarah's face.

Nicole was dead and Sarah would be if he couldn't find her. But Jude didn't know where to look any more than he did when he began searching for Nicole. He needed help, and this time there was only one place left to turn.

*Lord, You've got to help me find Sarah.*

Sarah moaned. Her head pounded as if someone were driving a jackhammer through her skull.

As she blinked open her eyes, the room swirled around her. Where was she?

She tried to rise from the bed she was lying on, but her hands were tied to the bedposts. She tugged against the restraints. They held firm.

Panic swept over her. She needed to stay calm so she could find a way out.

Her eyes flicked over the room. Ecru walls,

crown molding, a dresser with attached mirror. Heavy brocade curtains covered the window.

Was she still at Elena's house?

Rashad had been there. He'd grabbed Sarah. She remembered the sound of an engine, a sense of moving.

No, she wasn't at the Cunningham estate.

But where?

Footsteps sounded outside the room.

Her heart thumped hard. She closed her eyes, pretending she was still asleep.

The door opened. Someone stepped toward the bed.

Sarah forced her breathing to remain even, rhythmic.

"Don't you worry, Sarah. I told Rashad I'd stand guard, but I won't let him hurt you. Soon as you wake up, I'll find a way to get you out of here."

The voice sounded familiar.

When she heard the person shuffle away from the bed, Sarah cracked her eyes open.

Roy Valentine.

Could she trust what he'd said? Would he be able to protect her from Rashad?

Despite her efforts to remain alert, her eyes grew heavy and she drifted back to sleep.

A crash awakened her sometime later.

Roy's voice. "Don't you—"

Another crash.

Sarah thrashed at the restraints, trying to free herself, but she was too weak to pull out of their hold.

The door opened. This time her eyes were wide with fear as the intruder entered the room.

Tall, lean.

Damian.

"What'd you do to Roy?" she demanded.

Damian laughed. "Look at you. Tied to the bed and acting like you're in charge." He shook his head, eyes cold as ice. Then he shoved his thumb to his chest. "I'm in charge. You answer to me now."

"Untie me, Damian."

"What about Brittany?"

"She's making a new life for herself, one that doesn't involve you."

"Why you—" He raised his hand to strike her.

Roy stumbled into the room and grabbed Damian's arm. "Leave her be."

He pushed the older man aside. Roy crashed into the nightstand, the lamp wobbled and a vase toppled onto the floor.

Sarah saw a glint of steel. "He has a knife."

Damian jabbed the blade into Roy's rib cage. Air wheezed from his lungs.

Raising his hand, Damian struck again. Blood

splattered against the wall as Roy crumbled to the floor.

The tall, lanky street punk sauntered toward the bed, and the room filled with Sarah's scream.

# FOURTEEN

Jude raced to his truck. In the distance, sirens wailed. The police and EMTs would be at the warehouse in a matter of minutes. Bull could hold everything together until they arrived.

Jude had to find Sarah, and only one place came to mind. He stuck the key in the ignition, shoved the truck into gear and stomped on the accelerator.

Tiny pellets of ice hammered the windshield. He forced the defroster and wipers to high and headed north to the Highlands.

Traffic was light. If what Bull had said was true, the inclement weather had Atlanta spooked. Jude increased his speed, taking advantage of the relatively empty streets.

Despite the lack of cars on the road, it seemed an eternity until he pulled into the lot in front of the three-story apartment complex where Nicole had lived.

*Lord, don't let me arrive too late.*

Like a crazed man, he raced up the sidewalk, pushed the buzzer to every apartment, counting on at least one of the tenants to grant him entrance.

His hunch paid off. The outer door buzzed open. Jude ignored the elevator and opted for the stairs, taking them two at a time to the third floor.

Exiting the stairwell, he checked the hallway. Empty. Pushing forward, he found Nicole's apartment and stormed into the living area, ignoring the fact that someone, anyone could be waiting for him.

If Rashad had grabbed Sarah, surely he'd have one of his men standing guard.

Damian perhaps?

The way Jude felt, he'd rip the punk in two if he had done anything to hurt her.

The upscale apartment looked exactly the same as when he and Sarah had talked to Tonya.

No sound. No indication—

Then someone moaned.

"Sarah?"

Jude crashed through the bedroom door. His eyes flicked over the rumpled sheets. The bedside lamp was overturned. A vase lay broken on the floor. Next to the cracked porcelain, he spied a trail of blood.

"Sarah?" he screamed again.

Dark red droplets led to the adjoining bath.

He pushed the door open. A man lay facedown on the tile floor. Blood was smeared across the sink and splattered over the tile.

The guy coughed. Jude reached for his shoulder and turned him over.

"Roy?"

His eyes blinked open. He tried to speak. "He… he got Sarah. I tried to protect her."

"Who's got her?" Jude demanded.

"Damian."

Jude's gut tightened. "Where'd he take her?"

"A friend told me Damian's got a place, south of 285," Roy mumbled. He gave Jude directions. "House sits this side of the railroad tracks."

Roy grabbed Jude's arm, his grip strong in spite of his injury. "He'll overdose her, then dump her body in some back alley. The cops will never be able to prove he did it."

Jude reached for the phone, relieved to hear a dial tone, and called 911. "Send an ambulance," he said to the operator.

"I'll be okay," Roy assured him. "You go on. Find Sarah. She was nice to my grandmother. Told her how to get help for Shawn."

Pulling a towel from an overhead rack, Jude shoved the thick terry cloth against Roy's side. Then he repositioned the man's belt and cinched it over the chest wound, creating a makeshift tourniquet that appeared to work.

"I'll get help." Jude ran to the apartment across the hall and pounded on the door until a man answered.

"There's a guy in 3A. He's hurt. Stay with him until the ambulance arrives."

With the neighbor watching over Roy, Jude double-timed down the stairs and into the cold afternoon. Snow covered the street, and a mix of sleet and snow pelted his face as he raced for his truck.

Jude had to find Sarah before it was too late.

Sarah was piled like a rag doll on the back seat of Damian's Eldorado. Her head throbbed and her mouth was dry as cotton. The rope he had used to tie her wrists cut into her flesh, but she continued to work her hands back and forth, hoping they'd pull free.

A wave of nausea mixed with fear roiled over her as the car braked to a stop. Damian yanked her out into the cold. She twisted her head, frantically searching for any sign of another human being.

She saw nothing except the blinding snow and the railroad tracks that ran behind the small clapboard cottage.

A speck of a farmhouse sat on the horizon beyond the tracks. Smoke rolled from its chimney.

Someone must be home, but too far away to hear her cry for help.

"Don't do this," she demanded, causing Damian's grip to tighten on her arm.

He shoved her along the icy path, through the back door of the house and into the cramped kitchen.

An oak table stood in the center of the room, the top cluttered with mason jars and plastic tubing. Jugs of chemicals sat on the floor.

Sarah read the labels. Muriatic acid, acetone, Red Devil Lye.

The place reeked. She coughed, trying to clear her lungs.

Evidently, Damian was cooking up his own batch of meth.

Yanking a chair from the table, he shoved her down.

"Please, Damian—"

"Shut up." He raised his hand and slapped her face.

Her cheek burned and tears stung her eyes. She blinked them back, determined not to let him see her cry.

Wind whistled through the doorjamb and swirled around her. Somewhere along the way she'd lost her coat, and she shivered in spite of her desire to remain strong.

Damian picked through the clutter on the table until he found a plastic bag full of white powder that he placed on the counter. Opening the overhead cabinet, he pulled out a one-inch strip of rubber.

Frantically, she tugged at the ropes that bound her hands, feeling a surge of elation when the thick hemp loosened ever so slightly.

"Damian needs a little something to make him feel real good before he decides what he's gonna do with you." He laughed, a maniacal sound that sent chills scurrying down her spine.

*God, help me,* she silently prayed.

He found a syringe in the drawer by the sink and pushed up the sleeve on his left arm to expose scraped, torn flesh.

Rubbing his fingers gently over the angry wound, he sneered at Sarah. "Look what that army dude friend of yours did to me. Only, now I've got something he wants."

Her eyes grew wide. "What do you mean?"

Damian tapped some of the white powder into a spoon he grabbed from the sink and added a few drops of water.

"He'll come looking for you, but he'll be too late."

Too late because she'd be overdosed on the heinous concoction brewed in this filthy kitchen.

She twisted her hands against the rope. Her flesh

was raw, but she ignored the pain. Relief swept over her as one hand pulled free, then the other.

Damian's attention remained focused on the white powder.

Sarah didn't have time to wait for a better opportunity. She leaped from the chair and ran for the door. Her fingers grabbed the knob.

Damian dropped the spoon and lunged for her. Raising his hand, he struck her face. The blow threw her against the door. She grabbed hold of the nearby counter, trying to remain upright, hearing the crunch of tires driving over the newly fallen snow.

Jude turned down a two-lane back road and made a quick right onto the dead end Roy had told him about.

In the distance he spied the railroad tracks, then the small clapboard cottage. The gold Eldorado sat out front. From the looks of the tire tracks, the car hadn't been there long.

Jude screeched the truck to a stop and jumped to the ground.

The cottage door flew open.

Damian stepped from the house, his left arm wrapped around Sarah's neck. He held a gun in his right hand aimed at her head. She stumbled, struggling to free herself from his hold.

"Look who's here," Damian shouted into the wind. "I knew you'd come for Sarah."

Her eyes were wide with fright. Had he hurt her?

"Let her go, Damian."

The punk shook his head, his grip tightening around her neck. She grimaced and clawed at his arm.

"This is between you and me, Damian. No reason to get Sarah involved."

"I was fixing her something to make her feel real good. You want a little of my special batch?"

Relief swept over Jude. Damian hadn't given Sarah any drugs. At least not yet.

In the distance a train whistle blew.

Jude edged closer. "Turn her loose."

"You're a fool to think I'm gonna do that."

Jude sent Sarah a reassuring glance. If only something would throw Damian off for a second.

Understanding registered in her eyes. She turned her head ever so slightly. Damian's arm slipped up a fraction of an inch. Sarah opened her mouth and sank her teeth into the bruised flesh on his forearm.

He howled with pain. For an instant his grip eased. Sarah twisted out of his hold. Stepping back, she turned panic-stricken eyes questioningly toward Jude.

"Run!" he screamed.

She stumbled away. Damian followed close behind with Jude in pursuit.

Her foot slipped on the icy ground. She went down on one knee, righted herself, then struggled on.

Damian grabbed her arm. She jerked out of his hold.

Jude tackled him from behind. Damian collapsed onto the icy ground. The gun slid out of reach.

Jude pounded his fist into the punk's jaw. He rolled away from Jude, righted himself and grabbed a knife from his belt. Blade extended, he staggered toward Jude.

The sound of the train grew louder.

If Sarah crossed the tracks ahead of the engine, Damian wouldn't be able to follow until the train had passed. Enough time to get to the farmhouse Jude spotted sitting on the horizon.

"Sarah, run to the farmhouse. I'll hold him back."

Damian slashed the knife into Jude's ribs, the tip of the blade ripping through his flesh.

Jude gasped and grabbed his side. Damian reached for Jude's arm and twisted it behind his back.

In that split second, the past flooded over him. He was a boy again. The car had stalled on the tracks. They had all escaped when his mother raced back. Jude tried to run after her, but his father's strong arms held him in place.

The realization slammed through Jude. His father couldn't save his mother because he had to save his son.

The chilling cry of the train's whistle cut through the cold and snapped Jude back to the present. He jerked free of Damian's grasp. The punk swung the knife again. The blade scraped Jude's shoulder.

He landed a fist in Damian's gut. Air whooshed from his lungs. Damian doubled over. The knife dropped from his hand as he collapsed onto the frozen ground.

Sarah turned to look at Jude.

The train roared closer. The whistle shrieked a frantic warning.

"Keep going," he screamed. She had to make it to the other side.

"Damian's got a gun," Sarah yelled, her voice barely audible over the roar of the train.

Jude glanced over his shoulder.

From where he lay, Damian fumbled with his leg holster and pulled out a revolver. He raised the gun and fired.

White lightning exploded into Jude's left arm. He flinched but kept moving.

Fat drops of blood splattered across the snow.

Sarah's face was stretched with fear, her eyes wide. She screamed Jude's name.

He raced forward, willing his legs to move faster. "Get across the tracks, Sarah."

"Not without you," she shouted back, stretching out her hand for him.

Another shot rang out.

Jude slipped, righted himself and surged on. Just a few feet farther and he'd reach her. She had to get to the other side.

*Please, God.*

The train's whistle mixed with the click-clack of the wheels, zipping along the tracks. The earth vibrated beneath him.

Jude grabbed Sarah's hand.

Towering over them was the gleaming steel engine. Behind them, Damian was less than a breath away.

They leaped.

The sound of screeching metal and Damian's last scream echoed in the cold, winter air.

# FIFTEEN

Sitting alone in the darkened chapel, Sarah heard the door open. She turned and smiled, then scooted over to make room on the small bench.

"What'd the doctor say?"

Left arm supported in a sling, Jude smiled back at her, then settled into the seat she offered.

"That you've been taking good care of me. Everything's healing. He said I'll be able to drive back to Fort Campbell by the end of my leave."

"I told the police how we jumped to safety just in time." She sighed, as if remembering all that had happened. "For an instant I…I didn't know if you'd gotten clear. The sound of the train was deafening. All I could see was flashing metal as it zoomed past."

He reached for her hand. "There was a moment when I didn't know if either of us would make it."

Sarah's fingers entwined with his.

"Any word about the shelter's financial situation?" he asked.

"The new accountant claims we'll be in the black by the end of the year."

"Did you talk to Cynthia?"

"She wants me to stay on and help her for as long as I like."

"Bull's staying, as well?"

Sarah smiled. "He and Cynthia seem to be connecting in a very special way."

"Now that's exciting," Jude said, genuinely happy for both of them.

Sarah pulled her cell phone from her pocket and dropped it into Jude's hand. "Didn't you tell me you needed to make a call? Talk as long as you like while I check on the kids."

After Sarah left the room, Jude clutched the phone, working his fingers over the smooth metal.

God had revealed the truth to him. Now he knew what had happened so long ago.

Flipping open the cell, he tapped in the digits.

An answering machine clicked on. "Please leave a message." His dad's voice.

All these years, Jude had it wrong. His dad hadn't been able to save his mother because he'd been holding Jude, keeping him from running back onto the tracks.

The answering machine beeped. There was so

much Jude needed to say. "Dad, I'm sorry." He sighed. "If you can forgive me, I'd like us to start over."

Jude snapped the phone shut and placed it on the bench.

Would his father be interested in renewing a relationship that had been so broken?

The door opened, and a hand touched his shoulder. Jude turned and looked into Bull's understanding eyes.

"Sarah told me she gave you her phone. How'd it go?"

"He wasn't home. I left a message."

"Give him time. He'll come around. Don't know any father who'd turn his back on his son."

"After the way I acted, I don't deserve to be forgiven."

Bull shook his head and pointed to the large central cross. "We're all forgiven, my man. You remember that."

Jude looked up. Christ had died between two thieves.

"What about Damian's funeral?"

"His brother's making the arrangements."

"The news report said Elena's been charged with Nicole's murder as well as Rashad's."

"Hard to believe," Bull said with a sigh. "But there is some good news. Nicole's grandmother called. Viki signed herself into rehab. Once she gets clean, she'll move in with Opal and Shawn."

Bull dug in his pocket and pulled out the gold heart-shaped money clip. "I happened to run into a friend of my brother's this morning. Told him how important this was to you." He dropped the clip into Jude's hand.

As the big man left the chapel, Jude looked down at the gold heart with the small cross etched on the upper left quadrant. His treasured keepsake from the past.

Sarah walked back into the room and reclaimed her seat. They sat in silence for a minute before Jude spoke.

"I came here looking for Nicole, thinking I loved her. But what I felt wasn't love. I was a lonely soldier on R&R, and Nicole gave me a couple weeks of attention. I'm convinced she wanted to get away from her life, just as I was trying to have some time away from the war and the stress of battle."

Jude took Sarah's hand. "Truth is, I've been running away all my life. From the memory of what had happened to my mother, from my father who didn't have a clue about raising a child alone."

Jude glanced up at the three crosses. "I was even running from God, whom I'd shut out of my life. When I came back to Atlanta, I said I was searching for Nicole. But in reality, I was searching for answers to my life."

Sarah nodded, her eyes filled with understanding. "The way I see it, if you hadn't been looking for Nicole, we never would have met."

Rubbing her fingers over his hand, she admitted, "I never allowed myself to fall in love. All those years, I had been blinded by a memory that wasn't true."

"Something we share in common," Jude said.

"Funny, huh? Once I realized I'd been wrong about my mother, I also realized I'd been wrong about not accepting love. Only, by then it was too late."

Jude frowned. "What are you saying, Sarah?"

"I'm saying I had already fallen in love with you."

Everything had come full circle. Jude had come back to Atlanta looking for true love. And he'd found it.

Slowly, deliberately, he lowered his mouth to hers. "I love you, Sarah Montgomery," he whispered just before their lips met.

# EPILOGUE

Church bells pealed overhead as Jude stood at the altar. His heart swelled with love for the beautiful woman at his side.

"I feel like a fairy princess in a storybook wedding," Sarah whispered. "You look so handsome in your dress blue uniform. I truly am marrying my Prince Charming."

Jude squeezed her left hand and looked down at the gold bands they both wore.

"You may kiss the bride," the minister said.

Jude took Sarah into his arms. His kiss was filled with the promise of all the future would hold for both of them.

Then turning, they faced the congregation. In the front right pew, Sarah's mother dabbed at the tears of joy running freely down her cheeks. Beside her, Hank smiled, his arm wrapped lovingly around his wife's slender shoulder. No doubt about it, the counseling was paying off.

From the front left, Jude's dad beamed like the proud father he was. He and Jude had spent time together, reflecting on the past, both asking forgiveness for the mistakes they each had made.

In the second row, Bull and Cynthia sat next to the kids from Hope House dressed in finery donated from Patrice's shop.

Keesha handed Sarah her bouquet of yellow roses as the military honor guard marched with precision down the aisle and came to a halt at the first pew. In unison they turned, raised their sabers and formed an arch overhead.

"Now I have the honor of presenting Captain and Mrs. Jude Walker," the minister announced.

Standing, the congregation clapped their approval as the organist began to play the recessional.

Jude nodded his appreciation to the men. Then he took Sarah's arm, and together they walked through the saber arch.

A new assignment to Fort McPherson in the heart of Atlanta would be Sarah and Jude's first home. After that? Only God knew.

One thing was certain. They would always have each other.

Jude felt the money clip in his pocket as they left the church and stepped into the bright Atlanta sunshine. He leaned close to his new bride and whispered in her ear, "I'll love you forever, Sarah."

"Are you sure?" she asked, her eyes playful.

"You know the answer," he said before their lips met. "Cross my heart."

\* \* \* \* \*

Dear Reader,

In *MIA: Missing in Atlanta,* returning war hero Captain Jude Walker searches for a woman he met on R&R. But she's disappeared, and Jude needs Sarah Montgomery's help to solve the mystery. Together they learn authentic love is grounded in truth, and memories of the past are not always as they seem.

Like the characters in this book, we can become burdened by old hurts that hold us back. If we give those situations to the Lord and ask for his help, we can be confident He'll lead us to a place of healing and peace.

I wrote this story when my son was deployed to Iraq for the second time with the 101st Airborne Division and have dedicated the book to the brave men and women in uniform who defend our nation. Please join me in praying for their safety. If you have loved ones deployed far from home, e-mail their names to me at *debby@debbygiusti.com* so I can add them to my prayer list.

Thank you for reading *MIA: Missing in Atlanta,* and be sure to visit my Web site, *www.debbygiusti.com,* for information about my next book from Steeple Hill.

Wishing you abundant blessings,

Debby Giusti

# QUESTIONS FOR DISCUSSION

1. Why does Jude run from the Hope House chapel on the night he meets Sarah? Explain why the three wooden crosses hanging on the wall trigger memories from his past.

2. How does Sarah show her love for the Lord through her outreach to the less fortunate? In what ways do you show your love for the Lord or how do you see that love manifested through the service of others?

3. Jude turned his back on his father and on his father's faith. Have there been times in your life when the actions of another have dampened your love for God? How did you find your way back to God?

4. How are Jude's idealism and sense of duty revealed throughout the story as he searches for Nicole? Did you find Jude to be a sympathetic character?

5. What causes Jude's change of heart when it comes to his relationship with the Lord? Have there been people in your life who have affected your outlook in a positive way?

6. Compare and contrast Sarah and Nicole, and explain how Jude eventually realizes authentic love is grounded in truth.

7. When we open our hearts to the Lord, miracles happen. How is that demonstrated through Bull's life? What about the other characters?

8. What significance does the heart-shaped money clip play in the story? Making a cross over our hearts means to promise; what could it symbolize to a person of faith?

9. Nicole wanted a better life for herself. How do you think Jude may have influenced her in that regard?

10. What leads Sarah and Jude to realize memories of the past are not always as they seem? Have you had similar experiences? If so, discuss one.

# *Love Inspired*
## SUSPENSE

## TITLES AVAILABLE NEXT MONTH

### Don't miss these four stories in April

**HIDDEN MOTIVE by Hannah Alexander**

Sable Chamberlain's grandfather is dead, and an ice storm
has her trapped with all the suspects. If Sable and her
coworker, Paul Murphy, can't solve the murder in time, they
won't be able to protect themselves from being next on the
hit list....

**IN HIS SIGHTS by Carol Steward**
*Reunion Revelations*

Despite the two suspicious deaths pushing Magnolia College
into the limelight, publicist Dee Owens is determined to
restore her alma mater's reputation. And now, thanks to
Dee's expert damage control, all eyes are on her—including
the murderer's.

**LAKEVIEW PROTECTOR by Shirlee McCoy**
*A LAKEVIEW novel*

When Jasmine Hart loses her family, her life shuts down...
until Sarah, her mother-in-law, asks for her help. Ex-military
man Eli Jennings is in town as a favor for a friend, but when
Sarah disappears, Jasmine and Eli must work together to
find her—and unravel the secret she's been keeping.

**WITNESS by Susan Page Davis**

There's no body and no evidence, but Petra Wilson still claims
she saw her neighbor strangle his wife. No one believes her,
except for private investigator Joe Tarleton...and the killer,
who is determined to silence the only witness.

LISCNM0308